Lords of Misrule

Maggie Rawdon

NOTE

Content information is available on my website at:
maggierawdon.com/content-information/

ONE

R owan

"Masks on boys. We're in and out on this one." I straighten my own gold Krampus mask and throw the burlap satchel over my shoulder. Tightening my grip on it with the black driving gloves I have on. We're dressed in all black from head to toe minus the masks to keep a low profile.

Tonight's the night we're collecting fucking dues on Professor Colin Mitchell. He's been betting a lot of money on our little side games and losing again and again. Always coming up with an excuse for why he doesn't have the money yet. Always using his rank as a professor as a shield to keep him from feeling the conse-quences. But Finn's in his class, and the good prof has bragged one too many times about the artwork he's got in his personal collection. So we're about to make it a little lighter.

"Fuck these things are creepy as hell." Hudson looks himself over in the mirror in our living room, the brown of his shaggy hair curls around the silver color of the mask. The three of us all play hockey for Vermilion, and we've lived together just off campus since sophomore year in this giant old Victorian. It's a notorious party house, haunted by the dead and the living, and the first place I've really been able to call my own.

"Yeah. That's the fucking point." Finn shakes his head, pulling his copper mask that matches mine down. He looks like something out of a nightmare. Finn's a massive guy, bulky six foot four, muscled and tattooed. He's the team's enforcer, and mine as well.

While Hudson's a newer addition, Finn and I have been friends since high school. Back when I was the poor scrawny weird kid who always got picked on. My grandparents offered to pay for me to play a sport if it'd help pull me out of my shell, and I chose hockey. That's where Finn and I met, and I assume he adopted me because he felt bad for me. The thing about Finn is he's a fists first, talk later sort of guy with more broken noses than he can count to show for it, but he has a soft spot for the broken ones.

Not that I'm broken anymore. Because now I run the books behind the scenes and the plays on the ice. We might not make the pros but that doesn't mean we're not getting out of college without a nice little nest egg to get us started.

And the first step to that is collecting our fucking dues.

"This is an in and out operation. I got the keycode to the house from the maid."

"You fucking would." Hudson laughs, always amused at the fact that I have a revolving door of one-night stands while he's still fucking pining for his long-distance girl.

I shoot him a look, and his amused expression drops from his face.

"We cross campus like we're just part of the rest of the revelry here tonight. Sneak in the house, grab the paintings off the wall, put them in the sacks, and get back here. No detours. No loud noises. No fucking around. In and out. Got it?" I look at both of them, their heads bobbing and eyes closing in agreement.

We need the fucking money from these paintings—whether we just use them as leverage over the professor or we sell them on the market is yet to be decided. Mostly because I still need to find someone who can fence them for us. Cars, drugs, cash, guns. Those are the kind of items I can move easily when I need to. Rare paintings aren't really in my wheelhouse, and my connections to people who can handle them are pretty fucking slim.

But I've got my own people I need to pay—including guys on the roster with coin-operated consciences who are only willing to throw a game if there's a nice payday at the end of it. So it's do or die tonight. If I can't throw games, I lose my control over the bets and the books. I can't pay the people who win. And then I'm the one who has bad people breaking into his house in the middle of the night to get their dues.

"We got it, Rowan. Let's go." Finn nods for me to lead the way, and we head out into the night.

It's fucking freezing this time of year and where an ocean breeze might bring in a little bit of warmth, the wind off the river just whips around your body and freezes you in fucking place. Our all-black outfits are only so warm. Meant more to conceal our identities than to run around singing Christmas carols tonight.

St. Nick's Day on campus is raucous as hell. It doesn't start until tomorrow, but some of the guys have turned it into a two-day party—one that starts on Krampusnacht. The last big one before everyone goes home for the holidays—assuming they have someone to go home to. Keg parties are raging on almost every block, bonfires are burning in front and back yards, and drunken carolers stumble down the street singing Jingle Bells out of key.

We jump the back fence and head down the alleyway to the road on the far side of campus, trying to go unseen. I hear the sound of a creaky back screen door slamming shut, and glass crashing against glass. I look up to see someone on their porch, chucking an empty bottle of vodka into the recycling bin before they light up their cigarette.

I could fucking go for one right now. I quit a couple of years ago. It was a nasty fucking habit of mine. One I picked up in high school and did me no favors on the ice. I tried not to smoke during the season and then finally quit when I could feel it in my times. Not that it fucking mattered since I'm not going to be playing much more anyway. Unless I pick up a recreational league and skate around with a bunch of middle-aged dads wanting to relive their glory days, I have a few months left before it's over for good. I shudder at the idea of being some washed-up has-been. Though the silver lining is that I could have a cigar when I want.

We finish our walk to the professor's house, largely unnoticed. The masks we wear blend in with all of the elves and Santas and other holiday creatures roaming the streets inebriated and disoriented. I stare up at the massive brick structure that sits on its own rampart among a row of other old city homes. Most of them are occupied by professors or coaches, but a few people, unrelated to the university, live here too for the prestigious ivory tower address.

Professor Mitchell is an unassuming man in what I'd guess are his thirties. I took a class with him in my sophomore year, and Finn's in his class now. We both started out pursuing arts degrees. Me because I wanted what I thought would be the easy way out, and Finn because he actually really loves art. The irony is that I practice less and still have about the same amount of talent as he does—the kind that isn't getting either of us into any galleries or earning us money if we aren't stealing it. Which is exactly why we're standing outside the man's home right now.

I hope the code to get into the house is right. The maid had been a long con when I started suspecting that the professor wasn't going to pay up the thousands of dollars he owes us, and Finn argued he had to have the money given the artwork he owns. I bumped into her at a local bar, struck up a conversation with the mousy little thing, and had her eating out of the palm of my hand by the end of the night. The first night wasn't a burden, but the weeks after when I had to pretend I gave a flying fuck about anything she had to say? That was more difficult. Pretending to date her and having to come up with ways to dodge all her requests to meet her parents and friends had been something akin to torture.

But it had gotten me access to her phone where she kept all her notes about the houses she cleaned. Where they kept the cleaning supplies, quirks they had about how they liked things, and most importantly codes to get into their homes and disable their security systems. Professor Colin Mitchell being at the top of that list with a note that he tipped well too. Another thing that makes me feel less guilty about taking what he owes.

"Take it from the rich. Give it to the poor," Hudson muses, more to himself than anyone.

"Don't you think that's a little fucking ironic?" Finn side-eyes him through his mask.

Hudson's rich as fucking Croesus. Or at least his family is back in New England. Where his girlfriend and the rest of the things he probably should be focused on are. But he ran off for a whole host of reasons I can't blame him for. The only problem is, now he just has an annoying habit of pretending he's poor while still walking around in designer shoes and clothes with a slowly depleting bank account that still manages to put the rest of ours to shame—not that it takes much. At least for now. But I have every intention of turning the fucking tables for all of us.

"Ironic? No. Poetic—yes." He hums before he starts up the steps.

The hairs on the back of my neck raise. I wanted to be sure there weren't any floodlights or other potential pitfalls before we went rushing up to the house, but apparently, we're just going to fucking Leeroy Jenkins this shit like a bunch of fucking amateurs.

Finn and I follow him up to the porch that wraps around half of the house. We walk around to the side door where the trees keep us obscured from the street and the neighbors. It's also where the entry keypad is. I glance at the windows one more time. The lights are all off and the house looks deserted. According to Finn, he has a conference to attend this weekend and is halfway around the country.

Hopefully, that means we're in and out. I quickly plug in the numbers to the security system, and the alarm gives a cooperative ding to let me know it's been disabled. Then I use the key the maid had on her chain, helpfully labeled with each house name she works at. I slide it into the lock, then a moment later the door's easing open, and we're slipping inside.

Despite a lot of petty criminal shit on my part, I've never actually broken into a home. I'm fucking shocked at how easy it is with the right kind of help. I take the first steps in, and Finn and Hudson follow. We've done some research ahead of time, and every time we work with a new client who wants to take bets, we make sure to shoot the shit with him. Or rather, Hudson does. That's his specialty. Finn and I could give a fuck less. But Hudson can talk to anyone anywhere about fucking anything. They don't even know what's happening, and they're buried in a discussion about annuities and municipal bonds or the state of golf courses at St. Andrews or whatever fucking shit rich people—or the hangers-on like Professor Mitchell—like to talk about.

It's a trove of information when Hudson digs in like that because it means we know about their pets, their home, their cars, their travel habits, and their family members—including who they're fucking. Luckily Professor Mitchell is one very sad, single, and lonely man without even a pet to keep him company. Which should make this whole affair even easier than I originally thought.

We slip through the kitchen and into the living room. Despite his lonely state, the man still has a Christmas tree that he's left the lights on. It sits just in front of the window, dimly lighting the room and illuminating the gold frames of the paintings on the wall. The ones he constantly brags to his students about. Ones worth a couple of thousand more than he owes us—interest and a penalty fee for making us retrieve them as far as I'm concerned.

"These the ones?" I turn to Finn to confirm.

"Yeah. Looks right. He's shown us them a few times in class."

"Frames are fucking fancy." Hudson runs his finger along the edge of one.

"They are. So don't get your grubby fucking hands on them," a female voice cuts through our muted chatter, and my blood runs cold.

Two

C harlotte

This is the last thing I need right now. Especially when I'm already taking care of Colin's whiny man-cold self. I have no idea how the hell I'm going to stop three masked men getting ready to abscond with *my* paintings. Or what would be my paintings once I'm done with Colin. Over my dead body did I put in all this work fucking my art history professor for nothing.

I've come down here to grab some more cold medicine for him after he skipped his conference to sniffle his way through the weekend in bed, begging me to bring him ginger ale and crackers while he watches old reruns of Antiques Roadshow on TV. He was having a coughing fit a few minutes ago and woke me up to get it. Because a simple cold means he's on his deathbed. Incapable of a feat so daring as to walk down the stairs in the night.

That job was left to me. Which is why I'm now staring at the backs of three men wearing all black, their faces covered with Krampus masks. One gold, one silver, and one a coppery bronze.

Apparently, they're medaling in being assholes. Or they've just skipped out on one of the raging St. Nick parties on campus.

They freeze for a moment after they hear my voice. I'm hoping they'll go running back to wherever they came from. Scared about being caught and scattering off into the night. That this is just a crime of opportunity. But when I see the gun tucked into the gold one's belt, I know I have way bigger problems on my hands.

I reach for it just as he does, but I'm faster—only by half a second, but it's enough. I rip it out and place the barrel against the back of his head, the muzzle buried in a mess of wavy dark brown hair.

"Ah, ah, ah," I tut. "Let's not do anything rash right now."

The guy in the silver mask inhales sharply, his eyes darting to the side to study me, confusion written in them. The one in the copper-colored mask moves suddenly, turning abruptly, and lunging in my direction. He's big. Bigger than both of the other guys, with muscular arms and shoulders that make him look intimidating, and at least half a foot taller than my five foot eight, probably more. It's hard to tell with those fucking horns.

I flick the safety and snap my eyes to his.

"Stop." The word is quiet but firm. I don't need Colin joining this little midnight party, but I need these assholes to understand I'm not fucking around. For his part, he freezes.

"I assume you're all friends, or at least co-conspirators in this little midnight adventure. So if you don't want your friend here to lose the back part of his skull, I'd suggest not making any more sudden movements. It'll do us all a favor because I don't want to have to clean brain matter off the paintings."

"So much for being fucking alone," the one in the gold mask growls, and the way Silver Mask winces, I'm guessing he's the one who failed the reconnaissance part of this mission. Not exactly his fault. Colin's and my situationship is a secret for a reason. Mainly because fucking a student is highly frowned upon and his wanting to keep that secret is exactly the kind of leverage I need to make my plan work. Except now we have three fucking witnesses.

The eyes behind the copper mask narrow at me, a flicker of green in them visible from the twinkling lights on the tree. They widen then, with something like recognition. His lips, visible under the snarled nose of his mask, part suddenly, and I don't like it. Not one fucking bit. This guy must know me from somewhere, and I don't like being in the dark.

"Take the mask off," I order him.

He shakes his head.

"Take it fucking off," I repeat, digging the muzzle into Gold Mask's skull.

He shakes his head again.

"If you think I won't shoot your friend here, you're wrong."

Another shake of this fucker's head, and I'm losing my patience.

"He'll be dead, and you'll be in handcuffs." I morph my face into a desperate bewildered look before I mimic the whine of a crying woman. "Oh, officer. I don't know what happened. I came downstairs and these men were here. It looked like they were trying to steal something. I screamed for help. They tried to grab me. I didn't know what they were going to do—kill me, rape me. I was so scared. The gun fell. I picked it up... I don't know. I've never used a gun before, officer. But somehow, somehow..." I fake another sob. "I pulled the trigger. I don't know how. I'm so sorry, officer. So sorry... Oh my god. There's *so* much blood!" I flutter my lashes and smile again. "Are you familiar with castle law or did you not get that far in school?"

"Take the fucking mask off," Gold Mask grunts, his voice is rough and deep—an impatient tone coloring his words.

"Listen to your boss." I nod to Copper Mask.

His gloved hands go to the mask, pushing it back off his face. I recognize him immediately, a whisper of apprehension tinged with want winding its way down my spine. And he knows it. A subtle smirk crosses his face despite the stress.

It's Finn Graves—if the piercing green eyes aren't confirmation enough, the slightly crooked nose from all the fights he gets in, on and off the ice, as the hockey team's enforcer will confirm it. Most girls know who he is because he's an infamous fuckboy. I know who he is because he's in half of my art classes, including Colin's, and I'm more than a little jealous of his talent and have been for years.

He's also one-third of a triad of assholes on the hockey team, which means I know what lies behind mask numbers two and three.

"Rowan and Hudson, I presume?" I raise an eyebrow at Finn.

A subtle shrug of his shoulder and the slow close of his lids confirms it.

"How does she fucking know who we are? You fuck her?" Hudson asks.

"Shut the fuck up," Rowan growls.

"We're in the professor's class together."

"Apparently, there are extra credit opportunities we didn't know about," Hudson muses, smiling as he pulls his mask back to get a better look at me.

Rowan moves to turn around, and I grind the muzzle into his occipital bone.

"This doesn't change anything. In fact, I'm pretty sure offing this one earns me a gold star as far as half of campus is concerned." I offer up a saccharine smile.

I can see Rowan's fists ball up and feel the tension rolling off him. He's dying to take a chance and try to drop me and the gun.

"What do you want?" Finn asks, a hint of his accent breaking through the only sign he's stressed. His eyes study me though, looking me over. He's only ever known me as the quiet one who sits at the back of the class just like him. Both of us are apparently surprised to find ourselves facing off in this situation.

"I want you to get out of this house. Quietly. Without waking Colin."

"On a first-name basis when you suck his dick then?" Rowan grunts.

"Does your friend want to live, or do you think he's dying to have a bullet lodged in his jaw?" I raise a brow at Finn, and Finn's eyes move from me to his friend. His brow furrows and there's a slight tick of his jaw. These two are thick as fucking thieves, so I assume he's explaining in their silent language that I might actually mean what I'm saying.

And I do mean it. I don't want to deal with blood on the floor and cops in the house tonight. I just want to get Colin his cough medicine and go back to sleep, but if the alternative is losing these paintings—blood and cops it is.

"Charlotte?" A strained voice comes from upstairs, followed by hacking.

Fuck.

I look at Finn and Hudson, pressing my lips together in a sign for them to stay quiet.

"Be right up. Just spilled some of the cough syrup. Didn't want to stain the floor. I'll be there as soon as I get this cleaned up."

"Okay." Another cough is followed by the clearing of his throat.

I look back at Finn and Hudson, their eyes drifting up toward the ceiling, listening to his retreating footsteps.

"Leave and we can pretend like this never happened."

"He owes us money." Hudson frowns.

"Shut the fuck up, Hudson." Another growl from Rowan.

"How about it, Boss?" I tap Rowan with the gun.

"I'm not making any fucking deals with someone I can't see."

I roll my eyes.

"Walk toward the wall." I nudge him with the gun, and he takes a step forward. "All the way and keep your hands where I can see them."

He takes a few more steps and then stops, at least smart enough to follow my directions.

"Turn, slowly." I glance at Finn, but he hasn't moved, and Hudson's still rooted in place behind him.

Rowan turns around, looking demonic with his mask still on his face.

"You gonna get trigger-happy if I take this off?" he gripes.

"No."

Just like Finn, he wears driving gloves. They're distractingly fucking sexy on him. More so than Finn even. In part because he has really fucking nice hands. I would know. I had them up my skirt once while playing a ridiculously immature game of Seven Minutes in Heaven in my co-ed dorm sophomore year. He was drunk and high, so I doubt he remembers. I don't expect the same recognition I see in Finn's eyes, and I don't get it.

Just a nasty snarl of his lip as his eyes drift over me, no doubt irritated that a woman in Christmas-themed PJ shorts, a lacy tank top with no bra, and a messy bun is ruining all of his better plans. Probably not the kind of person he expected to be threatening him with his own gun.

"Charlotte, is it?" His eyes drift back up my body, stopping briefly at my chest and then lifting to meet mine. "Why the fuck would I just walk away when you know who we are? What's to stop you from running and crying to your sugar daddy upstairs?"

"If I wanted to tell him, I just had my chance."

"Why didn't you?"

"That's my business. Your business is getting out of this house alive."

A snort leaves him, and he shakes his head, his eyes drifting past me to survey the room while he thinks. I can see the cogs turning, trying to think of some way he can get out of this situation and still get what he wants. He's used to having things his way. People falling in line to make him happy. He's the captain of the hockey team and a silent figurehead on campus. He doesn't have to use many words to get what he wants most of the time.

I use the opportunity to take him in and get a good *long* look. Because Rowan is an ethereal sort of gorgeous. A cut jaw, slightly hollowed cheeks, lush lips, and an imposing brow that frames eyes that are a hauntingly pale gray. His forehead is damp with sweat from the mask and some of his dark brown hair curls over it.

"Give me the gun back, and we'll go."

"Do I look fucking stupid to you?"

He takes a step forward, a sneer marring his perfect face.

"Putting a gun to the back of my head makes you pretty fucking stupid."

"Your gun. After you broke into my house."

"Your house now?" His eyes light with the taunt.

"The house I'm staying in. None of this would have happened if you'd stayed at whatever frat party the three of you got drunk enough at to think this was a good idea. Who put you up to it? Some fucking bet on the hockey team?"

"Your fuckbuddy owes me money. Claims he doesn't have it." Rowan shares more than I expect him to after telling Hudson to shut up.

"And you told him these were here?" I ask, looking at Finn.

His eyes shift to the side, a half-shrug in acknowledgment. I shake my head, pretending to be disappointed but frankly a little amused that Finn and I think alike. Right before I think about what a moron Colin is for bragging about his money like this. Or going into debt to a fucking student. Or fucking one... Really it all fucking lines up for him. How he managed to get this far in life is a mystery. More brains than sense.

I need to get back upstairs with his cough medicine before he starts deciding the trip downstairs is worth it.

"Well, you'll have to find a different way. Now get the fuck out."

"What's to stop you from calling the cops?" Rowan glances at me.

"You'll just have to trust me."

"Fuck that," he spits.

"You don't have an alternative. Get out. Go back to your

party. And all of us can forget this." I motion toward the door with the gun, my eyes shifting to it and back to him.

He looks back at me, and I can tell he's ready to argue when Finn grabs his arm and tugs him. It's uncharacteristic and the movement seems to shock even Rowan who looks confused but follows Finn's lead. The three of them get to the door, Hudson making his way out before Rowan turns back.

"We're not finished."

"If you say so." I offer him another false smile, and Finn nudges him over the threshold, glancing back at me once before he follows Rowan out the door.

Three

F inn

"So much for your fucking research," Rowan cuts into Hudson as soon as we're down the block. "Could have gotten us all fucking killed by that psycho bitch."

"You can't expect me to know that he's secretly fucking a student," Hudson defends himself.

"No? You couldn't find a fucking rumor? No way that shit stays quiet. Someone always finds out and talks."

"Then they're particularly careful."

"Which is suspicious as fuck. She's got a tenured professor between her thighs, and she's not telling *anyone*?" Rowan shakes his head. "Nah. That doesn't make fucking sense. She's up to something."

"If you need this level of information, you need more. Someone who can hack his phone or his cloud or wherever the fuck he'd keep that kind of info on her," Hudson explains as we make our way down the street. "That's beyond my skillset."

"And you. Why the fuck are you so quiet? You're telling me you're in his class with her and you never figured out anything?" Rowan turns his anger on me.

"No. She's quiet. Sits near the back by me. We've had classes together for years since we're both art majors. I really thought she was..." I go quiet, realizing what I'm about to say doesn't help the situation.

"What?"

"A good girl. That whole... everything that just happened. Would have never fucking guessed. So I guess I had her all fucking wrong." I can't stop the smile that comes to my lips, forgetting for a minute that the mask doesn't shield that part of my face.

"Yeah. That fucking amuse you?" Rowan gripes, his tone slightly softer with me.

"No." I straighten my face. Letting on that I kind of like the girl who just had a gun to the back of his head is probably not going to help her or me.

"Good. Because it's not fucking funny. That was our best shot to get those paintings. I don't have a plan B."

"We'll figure it out. A sleep or two. It'll all come together again. Maybe she can help us." I shrug.

"Did she seem like she was wanting to help?" Rowan tilts his head at me, and the way the light flashes across the gold of his mask and dances off its horns has him looking like he might drag us all to hell right now.

"No. But she could have done a lot worse. Called the cops. Called for the professor. She went easy on us," I counter.

"You didn't have a loaded gun to the back of your head," Rowan argues.

"Life flash before your eyes?" Hudson asks, turning around to look at us for a moment and walking backward to accomplish it.

"*Your* life flashed before my eyes. For getting us fucked like this." Rowan shakes his head. "You realize she has everything now. Knows who we are. Has my gun. Can hold it all over our heads."

"Relax." Hudson smiles. "I don't think she wants to do that."

"Based on what?"

"I don't know. The way she was. Seemed like she just wanted peace. Didn't seem like she was particularly happy with the professor either." Hudson offers his opinion to the group and Rowan takes it in stride.

"Who would be? You've been around Mitch enough to know he's dull as fuck and even more self-absorbed. I'm sure he's just as bad in bed," Rowan muses.

"Didn't she just have a gun to your head?" Hudson smirks under his mask.

"Yeah. Doesn't mean she couldn't be a good fuck. Crazy ones are always good in bed." Rowan returns the sentiment.

I feel my stomach swirl at the thought of her going to Rowan instead of me. I'd had a small crush on her before. I could admit that. But the woman I just met? The one who was a ballbuster who could wield a gun and cut Rowan down to size with her words? It's hard to not be at least a little interested. But I can't be at odds with Rowan over her, and I definitely don't want to end up in jail because I got fucking lovesick over a girl I barely know.

One thing's for sure. It's going to make class on Monday interesting as fuck.

———

When I get to class, I see her sitting at the back like she always is. Her eyes are down on her phone, and she seems engrossed in whatever she's doing there. It's not until I sit down next to her that her lashes flutter briefly in my direction, right before they land straight back on her phone. But I can tell from the way she sits and the slight change in her breathing that she's hyperaware of my presence now.

"Have a good weekend?" I ask when she continues to pretend like I don't exist.

She looks up finally, briefly making eye contact before she looks to the front of the room where the professor is still missing.

"It was okay."

"Mine was interesting."

"Was it?" She continues to smile but her eyes warn me not to say anything that could compromise her in this class.

"It was. This girl I've known for a long time turned out to be very surprising."

"Yeah? She do that thing with her tongue?" She smirks at me.

"Not quite, although I think you'll have to tell me more about that." I grin at her.

"Well, maybe you didn't know her as well as you thought you did."

"Maybe. Maybe I want to know her better."

"Sure your friend's on board with that idea? He might not like her very much after the weekend."

"Oh, he doesn't. But he might come around under the right circumstances."

"Charlotte and Finn, do you have something you want to share with the class?" Professor Mitchell interrupts our conversation, and I'd been so involved with her that I hadn't even noticed him come into the room.

"No. I'm sorry, Professor." Charlotte's smile falters, and her eyes go down to her desk again.

"Good. Then let's get started on the works of Marie-Louise-Élisabeth Vigée-Lebrun, shall we?" Professor Mitchell announces and his eyes fall on me like he's assessing me before he looks back at his computer again and starts the lesson. I'm starting to wonder if this is the reason why no matter how well I do in his class, I never seem to get above a B.

She glances over at me one last time, an apologetic smile on her face and it makes me grin in return before I put my focus back on taking notes. I'll have to be careful with her. She's dangerous to me in more ways than one.

Four

harlotte

When I get home that night, I slip out of the diner T-shirt and pants I have on, tossing them in the laundry basket before I pull my hair out of my bun and shake it loose, rubbing my scalp for good measure. I reach for the clasps at the back of my bra, releasing them and tossing it on the side of the hamper. I need to do laundry. I need to find time to do laundry. But between homework, the diner, and keeping Colin entertained, I don't get much time for anything else.

I start to go for my panties, thinking I might hop in the shower before I crash on my bed when my heart nearly jumps out of my chest at the sight of a shadow in the corner of my room.

"Shame that you waste all that on Mitch."

It's Rowan. I'd recognize the slight rasp in his deep voice anywhere. He's sitting in the chair in the corner of my room, legs spread wide as his eyes drift over my body in the dim light. Amusement dances over his face as he leans forward on his elbows for a better look. His face catches the light when he does it, lighting all the perfect angles.

I fold my arms over my chest, covering my breasts even though it's useless since he's already had a good look. I will myself to look calm, stay calm, *be calm*. Because he's the kind of person who senses weakness and latches on to it. It's exactly how he got Colin in his debt.

"Yeah? Should I waste it on boys my age instead?"

"Less about age and more about competence."

"He's perfectly competent," I lie.

Rowan smirks, his eyes wandering again.

"I'm sure that's exactly why you keep a vibrator in the drawer and another in your overnight bag."

Fuck. He searched the room for his gun and probably any other information he could find on me.

"Did you find what you were looking for?" I know he hasn't because I put the gun somewhere for safekeeping, and the room I rent in this house isn't it.

He makes a face, acknowledging what we both already know. I doubt he'd even be here if I'd left it here for him to find.

"Your roommates don't seem to know you very well. They bought the story that I was your boyfriend wanting to leave you a surprise. Not very good security for someone like you."

"I normally don't deal with assholes like you."

He stands, taking several steps toward me. I hold my ground, letting him get so close I can feel his breath on my skin. He reaches out with a gloved hand and sweeps some of my hair behind my shoulder.

"Nah. You prefer assholes like Mitch. Or maybe you just tolerate guys like him so you can make a little extra cash on the side of your diner job."

He's definitely searched the room for information. I'll have to try to figure out exactly how many clues he has now.

"Maybe you need someone who can actually make you come hard." He takes another step forward and the backs of my knees hit the edge of the bed as I take one backward. His eyes light when my body jolts with the contact.

"And you're that someone?" I force a self-assured smile onto my face, one that taunts him.

He reaches out, grabbing my jaw, the leather brushing over my skin as his eyes study mine and then drift down over my face.

"We both know I am." He smirks before his eyes snap up to meet mine. "How did you put it again that night in the closet? 'Oh god. That was the first time. I've never come like that before.' That's what you said when you came all wet and messy on my fingers, right?"

And his memory is back. Somehow, he remembers that night sophomore year. I must have looked familiar, and he racked his brain until he figured it out. Not too drunk after all.

Double fuck.

I do my best to keep my stare blank. Any twitch or deviance is going to give me away and my body is already reacting to him. His voice, his hands, the unapologetic way he touches me. I have a fucking weakness for it, and it's going to be a real problem if I want to get out of this ahead. So I need to do something—anything—to get him off my back. Luckily, I can bluff with the best of them.

"I remember you running off like a little bitch after. Was it too much listening to me? Feeling how tight I was? Did you come too soon and make a mess?" I pretend to make a sad face. "Hope you don't embarrass yourself in front of other girls like that."

I get a tight-lipped smile in return.

"Still that hurt you missed getting my cock all these years later?"

"Still this disappointed in abilities that don't live up to the reputation."

"You caught me on a busy night. I'm happy to give you an updated demonstration. One that ends with my cock deep inside that tight cunt of yours. We can fuck the bitch out of you."

"Can Finn join?" I say it to shock him, but if I'm being

honest every fantasy I've had since the night of the attempted robbery has involved the two of them. Especially in all black with those masks. Fucking me face down on the ground, taking turns. Sometimes with Hudson joining in. My vibrator's been doing overtime just to try and keep up with how well that particular one works for me.

Another tight smile before his eyes go dark and his fingers dig into my jaw.

"Where the fuck is my gun, *Charlotte*?" He's remembering my name too. A thing I thought he might forget in the chaos. I assume I have Finn to thank for that.

"Not here."

"Where. Is. It?" His eyes narrow.

"So you can blow my brains out? Use my fingerprints to set me up for suicide? No."

"Is that what *you've* been planning?"

"I'm not planning anything. I've let you—and your friends— go without a word after you tried to rob a tenured professor."

"Out of the goodness of your heart, I imagine."

"Out of my need for a drama-free evening."

"You know I'll figure it out. It's a matter of time. You might as well tell me."

"There's nothing to figure out."

"Good. Then all we need to do is arrange a night you won't be at Mitch's. We get the artwork. You get the drama-free evening you want so badly. Right?"

"No."

"No?"

"I'm not going to let you just steal from him."

"You in love with him?"

"Maybe." I shrug.

I'm absolutely not. In the beginning, I found him somewhat charming in an offbeat sort of way. I really believed he liked me at first, but the more time went on the more I realized he didn't care about me. Just about what I could do for him. It's better this way given the plans I have in mind for him—made the job harder, but the decision easier.

Rowan's eyes search my face, a look of mild disbelief replaced by irritation and a hint of amusement.

"I'll figure out what it is you're after with him, and when I do, I'll make sure I bring it all down on top of you in the messiest fucking way possible. The longer you drag this out, the worse it'll be. Give me the gun. Stay out of our way with the paintings. Then we can both fuck off to where we came from. Simple."

"What are you even going to do with the paintings once you have them? Put them on your wall?"

"Do I look like a fucking art collector?"

"No. So what's your plan?" I challenge him. I doubt this asshole has put one iota of thought into how this plays out beyond the fact he wants them.

"My plan is none of your fucking business."

"You can't sell them the way you might other things. They're not an easy sale. You realize that right? They're unique and well-documented, and you'd need to find the right buyer who both wants them and is willing to take them without papers. Or you have to be able to make it look like it's not coming with sketchy provenance. Faking legitimacy is complicated and expensive. You have a plan for all that? Because I doubt it."

"You volunteering to help?"

"I'm willing to be the person who tells you you're out of your depth on this one, and if you get it wrong you and all your friends will go to jail. Do not pass go. Do not collect two hundred thousand dollars. Just you trying to phone home to beg for more money so you can trade commissary items to get the things you want for the next ten years."

"You've spent a lot of time thinking about this."

"You haven't thought about it enough. You have no clue what you're doing and not a single connection to pull it off."

His eyes light with realization, and his lips pull to one side as he studies me.

"Because you want to steal them for yourself." He scoffs. "How did I fucking miss it? Of course that's why you'd let us go. Why you're keeping that boring fucker so close."

"Why would I want to steal them?" I try to sound incredulous, but I feel my heart start to pound fast and heavy in my chest.

"I don't know. It doesn't really matter. But now I see why you wanted to stop us and keep it quiet. You wanted us out of your way, without drawing any extra attention." He shakes his head in amusement. "I kept saying it was odd you didn't scream for the professor. That you didn't call the cops and play out your damsel in distress routine for them like you threatened to. I thought it might have been because you wanted Finn. But now... *now* it all makes sense."

"I was kidding about Finn," I say defensively, wanting to change the subject and also wanting to rid him of ideas about Finn. I don't need Finn thinking I'm one of the dozens of women on campus crushing over the sound of his name. Even if I am.

"I'm sure you were." Rowan's self-satisfied smile spreads. "I bet your professor would find that interesting. Knowing you're imagining the hockey team's enforcer between your thighs when you're fucking him. Might bruise his ego enough, and you wouldn't be in a position to steal those paintings out from under him. I might be saving him heartbreak and trouble."

"Heartbreak," I scoff. Colin was a lot of things, but in love with me was not one of them. He liked fucking, and he especially liked fucking one of his students. The power he had over me and my grades. Being able to tell me not to wear panties to class and sit with my legs spread. It's a power trip for him. Not love.

"What's the matter? Couldn't convince him to fall with this cunt?" Rowan steps up to me and slides his hand between my legs. I feel leather brush over the insides of my thighs—his driving gloves again. Tight black ones that conform to every curve of his hands with black ribs on the knuckles. A thing he puts to good use when he presses one knuckle to the center of my panties, brushing over my clit through the cotton.

"I could teach you a thing or two. Give you some new tricks that would bring him to his knees."

"I'm sure you wish you could."

He brings his face a hairsbreadth away from mine—so close our lips are nearly touching.

"Or I could bring you to your knees. Would you like that better?"

I nearly bite my tongue to keep from saying yes.

"Fuck. Off," I say through gritted teeth.

"Oh, I will. To thoughts of my come dripping down this chin." His hand moves back to my face, running over my jaw again.

"Get out. Now." I shift my eyes to the door. I desperately need him gone before I do something stupid.

"We're not done. I *will* figure it out." He pulls away from me and heads for the door. My heart rate starts to slow again from the distance.

"Good luck."

"Sleep well." He smirks and then disappears out the door.

FIVE

H udson

That night Rowan comes home absolutely fucking pissed off. Throwing his phone and wallet on the table before he sits down across from me as I eat a late-night bowl of cereal and scroll my phone. I never know on any given day what sets him off. His temper takes a while to ratchet up, but once it's up, it's difficult to bring it back down.

"Rough night?"

"Still no gun."

"Went to see her, I take it?"

"She won't be moved, but I know why now."

"What's that?"

"She wants to steal them herself."

I drop my spoon into my cereal, setting my phone down to look up at him.

"*She* wants to steal them?"

"Yes. I don't know why. Or how she plans to do it."

"Or why she hasn't done it yet?"

"That too." His brow furrows as he picks at a dent in the wooden table.

"Maybe she hates him."

"Or maybe she needs the money."

"Maybe both?" I offer.

"Whatever it is, she has a million more chances than we do. She doesn't have to sneak in and out. She knows his routine. She fucking sleeps there regularly given how she was dressed. We're fucked, and I need the fucking money he owes me or shit's going to start falling apart fast. Assuming we could even get money for the paintings."

"Why wouldn't we?"

"She made some points I hadn't thought about."

I smile. I like her already, but that she can put Rowan in his place? I'm impressed.

"Stop fucking grinning like that. She's a pain in the ass."

"She's got a nice ass. Especially in those shorts she was wearing. What were her points?"

Rowan's lips flatten at my assessment of her.

"That if we don't do it right, we'll end up in jail. That we might not have the resources to do it right."

"Pretty big points." My brow furrows. I go along with most of Rowan's plans when it comes to our side hustle. He's cleverer than me when it comes to this stuff, and I've never had to live the way he and Finn did growing up. I never had to think the way he does. At least not yet. My time is running out on that front pretty fucking quickly. So I trust that he knows what's best. It just makes me nervous that these are things he hasn't thoroughly figured out.

"I didn't expect the professor to not pay up. Seems fucking stupid to go into debt to a student betting money illegally. I thought that would cover us with shit like this. And it has," Rowan argues defensively.

"Until now."

"Because he's too fucking stupid to know what's good for him."

"What if we worked with her?"

"With her?" He looks at me like I'm a fucking idiot.

"If she hasn't stolen them yet, maybe there's a reason. Something she's waiting on. Something she needs help with. She's just one person so maybe she needs help to get them out of the house or storing them."

"I doubt she wants our help."

"Not if you keep pissing her off," I admit and receive another flash of warning in Rowan's eyes.

"Have you gotten any more information on her?"

"I'm working on it. It takes a minute if I don't want to seem like I'm trying to stalk her."

"Stalk faster," he grouches. "In the meantime, I'll see what Finn knows."

"What I know about what?" Finn walks into the room at just that moment, headed for the fridge.

"Charlotte," I answer, Rowan's already busy scrolling his phone for something.

"Just fucking leave her alone, would you? It's awkward as fuck with her already in that class," Finn groans.

"She's going to steal the paintings," I interject when I see Rowan's face light like he's about to tear into Finn. They don't argue often, but when they do it's a fucking nightmare. So I do anything I can to avoid it.

"Charlotte's going to steal the paintings from Professor Mitchell? She said that?"

"Not exactly. It's not what she said. It's what she didn't say when I accused her of it. She looked guilty as fuck."

"But why?" Finn looks confused.

"Who the fuck knows. Does it matter? She's ten steps ahead of us already and she holds all the cards because she sucks his cock every night. We're fucked. I don't know how we fucking get out of it." Rowan sounds defeated.

"I suggested offering to work with her." I look to Finn, and his brow raises at the mention of it.

"But she doesn't trust us." Rowan shakes his head.

"She doesn't trust *you*. It's pretty obvious she trusts Finn. Or at least has a soft spot where he's concerned."

"She doesn't trust me. Especially not with Rowan in the picture."

"But the soft spot part?" I ask, wishing a little that it wasn't true. I have no business hoping for it. I have a girl even if she is long-distance and mostly absent from my life. I'm still loyal. Being jealous that a woman I just met wants my single friend is an exercise in stupidity.

"If it wasn't complicated, she'd probably fuck me. We've flirted back and forth in class for a while now. But it's complicated."

"So uncomplicate it," Rowan snaps.

"All right. I'll just get a time machine and make sure you never interact with her. That should solve the problem."

Rowan gives him the finger and kicks back in his seat, rocking on the back legs. It's a nervous habit of his.

"You could try to smooth things over with her," I suggest.

"She would see straight through it, and I like her. If she wants to come around and help us, that's going to have to be a discussion between her and Rowan. He can give her the facts of the situation and see if working with us seems like it's worthwhile to her. She'd respond better to that than manipulation."

"She'd respond better to that than manipulation." Rowan mocks me. "Jesus. Do you hear yourself?" Rowan shakes his head at Finn. "Don't you have someone we could work with, Mr. Fancy as Fuck?" Rowan turns his eyes on me.

"Someone we could work with?"

"Yeah. You've got lots of rich acquaintances who do rich people shit. I assume they buy paintings and sell them, right?"

"Yeah."

"So don't you know someone who moves them?"

"No. Most of them let their people handle it for them. They're not doing anything illegal, so it's not really a need of theirs."

"You sure?" Rowan presses.

"Again... to my knowledge, no."

"Even with your dad?" He raises a brow, and I feel the pang of shame I always do whenever my father is brought up.

"Even with my dad." Even though I had zero to do with any of it, I feel like I have to spend the rest of my life trying to fix things he did wrong. Ways my life was irrevocably fucked in a situation I had no say in.

"Let's just focus on how we can help her and maybe she'll help us," Finn interjects and gives me a sympathetic look.

"I'll focus on getting more information we can use as leverage on her. Hudson better too. *You* can focus on how you can help her." Rowan gives Finn a look. "And I mean without putting your dick in her."

Six

R owan

I'm sitting in the back of the diner Charlotte works at with my burger and drink, being waited on by one of her coworkers after she refused to serve me. Finn mentioned he thought she worked here when he saw a T-shirt with the diner's name stuffed in her bag, and I confirmed it when I found a paycheck in her room the other night. Now I want to know who she works with, who she talks to, where she goes after work, and how often she and the professor fuck. The more information I have on her, the better.

I have plans to twist and bend this girl until she breaks. Whatever I need to do to make sure that she eventually gets out of our way when it comes to Professor Mitchell. Because I owe a lot of people money. People who bet on our games. People who make final scores in games go the way I want. Cashouts that need to happen and a roster that needs to be paid so that I can continue to throw games in the direction that earns us money. I don't have time to play these games with her, even if some part of me is enjoying it.

I take another bite, checking my phone when I see an email pop up reminding me tomorrow's practice is canceled because they're fixing something in the arena. It's just as well because we need to lose this weekend. Not by too much, a small enough margin that it looks like it was a close game the whole time.

It's honestly more difficult to do than just losing or winning, especially when calls I can't control can swing the game in one direction or another. Paying off the officials has always been a goal of mine, but the initial outreach would be so incredibly risky I haven't tried it—yet. Although time is running low and Hudson's attempt to get information we can use as blackmail has been unsuccessful so far.

I glance out the window, one that has a view of more of the parking lot than the surrounding area and that's when I notice her. The long dark hair that fades into a violet color at the ends. She's standing against her car, another fact I know thanks to Hudson's renewed research, and a large bald man who looks like he lives off cigarettes and malt liquor is leaning over her. He's not quite yelling but it's obvious from his facial expressions that he's not amused with her.

Her face is placid, the only movement at all is the occasional wince when he leans in to point a finger in her face. He does it again, caging her in against the car. She holds her hands up, a pleading look on her face, but he doesn't cede any ground.

I'm trying to read what I can of either of their lips, using any context to try to discern if it's a boyfriend, another one she has on the line besides Mitch, or someone else to her. Before I can watch any further to get more clues, he closes in on her and she puts her hand out to stop him.

He snatches her wrist and wrenches it, her face twists with the pain, and I'm on my feet and making my way out the door. I don't know who this fucker is, but I'm about to find out. As fast as I move through the diner around a server and over a kid chasing crayons that fell on the floor, it's not fast enough. He's gone when I get out through the doors and into the parking lot. I spin around looking for him, but I don't see any sign. Not even a car pulling out onto the street.

Her car door is open, and she's sliding inside, shutting it behind her as I approach. She bends over the steering wheel, and I see her body rack with a sob. It makes my steps stutter to see her like this. She'd held three of us at gunpoint in her pajamas. She barely blinked when I showed up unannounced in the shadows of her bedroom. But now she's doubled over barely able to catch her breath from crying so hard. Whatever this fucker had on her, it must be bad.

I knock gently on the car window, but it still startles her, and she sits up suddenly, looking worse for wear when she sees it's me. She shakes her head.

"Fuck off." I can read the words more than hear them through the door.

I motion for her to roll the window down, and she shakes her head. I lean my forearms against the top of the car and get close, hoping she can hear me through the glass at this distance.

"I saw what happened. Let me in." Her eyes shift to the floor like she's embarrassed. So I do the thing I hate to do. A little bile rises in my throat before I choke it back. "Please."

There's a long pause, almost long enough to make me turn around before I hear the locks click, and she glances up at me. I round the car and open the passenger door, sliding in. She's silent at first, pulling down the visor to try to wipe away her tears and fix her makeup. I don't rush her. The last thing I need is to make her any more agitated than she is.

"What did you see?" she asks at last.

"Enough."

When she lifts her arm to fix her hair, I see the handprint still there. Red with scratches where that fucker's nails dug into her.

"Who was that?" I'm ready to murder him for marking her.

"No one."

"It's obvious the two of you know each other pretty damn well. A boyfriend? An ex? Maybe not happy you're fucking the professor..."

"None of the above. He doesn't even know about the professor."

"Does the professor know about him?"

"No. Of course not. You think he'd date me if he knew I had problems like that?"

"Does someone know? Someone who can help you if he comes back?"

"I can take care of myself."

"I'm well aware. But if he comes back—"

"Not if, when. And when he does, I'll take care of it myself like I always do. I don't need your help. He left, didn't he?" It's false bravado on her part because I watch her eyes scan the parking lot like she's double-checking to make sure he's really gone.

"What does he want?"

She sighs, shaking her head like she doesn't want to answer.

"So you can use it against me?" She huffs, a stuttered breath follows when she tries to take in a deep one. "I don't think so."

We haven't had a good start. Not that I really have a good start with anyone, but she's been a particular failure of mine on more than one occasion. So it's not exactly a surprise that she won't trust me.

"I need Mitch's paintings to cover a debt. I have a side business running bets on our hockey games. I owe good people money and a couple of dangerous ones too. If I don't get it soon... my accounts are in trouble, and then I'm in trouble. Mitch owes me probably at least what they're worth. He's been betting and losing and refusing to pay up. He thought he could fuck me over and get away with it. I need him to be wrong on that last bet." I tell the truth, hoping it's enough to get her to trust me. Or at least enough for her to open up and tell me what's going on and who this guy is. Her lips part and she looks at me, studying me like she's trying to figure out my angle in this.

"I was going to propose we work together. You obviously need them for something, and so do I. If we work together, maybe we make it happen. Maybe we don't. But probably better odds if we work together instead of against each other."

"Who says I need you?"

"The fact that you haven't taken them yet."

"I'm not planning to steal them." She shakes her head.

"Then what? Marry him and inherit them when he dies mysteriously on the honeymoon?"

She laughs. "That would be a good plan if he wasn't a prick."

"Then what?" It's my turn to study her. Wondering why she's continuing to go to this man's bed when she very obviously doesn't want to. Took care of him while he was sick and put up with whatever his bitchy fucking demands were. Then I realize again what I was so obviously missing. "Blackmail?"

Her fingers slide over the steering wheel, pausing to pick at a spot where the leather's peeling up.

"Yes."

"How? The relationship with the student probably won't be enough. It's fucking gross on his part, but you're of age."

"I was hoping if I waited long enough, I'd find something. He's gotten more and more bold with some of the things he says and does. And there are university policies."

"So threatening to report him and hoping he'll lose his job?"

"Without evidence... Without documenting it I don't know if it'll be enough. And I want to report him. Stop him from doing this to other women."

"If you blackmail him and then report him, what's to stop him from going after you then?"

"Nothing." She sighs.

"So what's more important?"

"I don't want other students to fall into his fucking trap. I want it to end with me. But I also need the money."

I take a breath, the puzzle pieces starting to come together. I follow her gaze out the windshield.

"Because you owe the guy that was yelling at you?"

"Yes."

"For what?"

"Freedom." She shakes her head, looking down again. "I don't owe him. My brother does." She lets out a loud sigh, slamming her hand against the steering wheel and looking over at me. "I don't know why I'm telling you all this. You'll just use it all against me. I'm a fucking idiot. Always trusting people I shouldn't."

"Why doesn't your brother make the money back? Is he around?"

"He has my brother, and he won't let him go until I pay him off."

"Pay him off for what?"

"My brother won't share all the details with me. I don't think I have the whole story. But my brother owes him. A lot of money and he's a cop so—"

"The guy that was out here is a cop?"

She nods. "Dirty as fuck, but a cop all the same."

Fuck me this girl is in deep.

"What was your brother doing that he tangled with a dirty cop?" It's a thing I've always tried to avoid. Successfully so far, but it seems like my time on that might be running out. Especially if this one thinks he can put his hands on her like he did.

"I don't know the details. Drugs obviously. Maybe more. Like I said Brady won't tell me everything. He's a fucking baby. Eighteen years old. He deserves a second chance. He only did the things he did to try to stay off the streets." Her tears start to flow again, and I'm fucking terrible at this part. I reach out and put my hand on her knee, rubbing a circle over it through the fabric of her jeans, trying to comfort her. She doesn't slap it away, so I assume it's helpful.

"How much do you still owe him?"

"10K. I've been trying to work more shifts when I can around school. Took out some loans to pay the first part and buy myself time. But it's not enough. I don't know if it'll ever be enough, and he's only given me six more weeks."

"Yeah. I get that." I glance over at the diner. It's dinner time and the place is barely alive. I doubt she makes enough tips to cover where she lives.

"So you see why I can't let you steal them." She eyes me, a steeliness in her green eyes that I can't argue with.

"I see why you feel that way."

"That's a non-answer if I ever heard one," she scoffs, grabbing a tissue out of her purse to clean up the mascara under her eyes as she sniffles.

"How much are the paintings worth? More than 10K I imagine?"

"Altogether on a normal market? Yes. Probably worth 30K or more each. But you won't be able to sell them in an open market. It'll be back-door deals. Middlemen who take a cut. Be lucky to get half that."

"You've done your research."

"I didn't go into this halfcocked."

I open my mouth to speak, and she shakes her head.

"Don't say anything about a whole cock."

"Don't have to now that you did." I smirk at her and get an exasperated look in response. But she doesn't cry again. She leans her head against the steering wheel, taking another breath before she stares up at the roof of the car.

"Fuck. I've told you way too much. I'm a fucking moron. Just remember when you fuck me over that you're sending an eighteen-year-old boy to his doom. One who probably wasn't all that different from you at that age." She glares at me, and something about it makes me want to kiss her.

The thought creeps down my spine and makes me shudder because I don't need this. Everything is complicated enough without having to worry about that. Especially not when she pisses me off as much as she interests me.

"I said I want to team up. Not fuck you over."

"And I'm supposed to trust you?"

"Do you have another choice now that you've confessed everything to me?"

"I guess not. But I don't want to get involved in all of your illegal stuff."

"Like stealing paintings and selling them?" I raise a brow at her.

"I mean the rest of it."

"I'm not asking you to. Fuck, I don't want you to be. That's all I'd fucking need."

"Okay. So then... I feel like you're being way too nice about this. What's the catch?"

"The catch is that we both need the money, so we're going to split whatever we make. Four ways between you, me, Finn, and Hudson."

"So I lose three-fourths of the money. Doesn't sound like a very good deal."

"You'll have help. Backup in situations like the one you had today."

"Assuming you're around. But hopefully if I agree, you won't be stalking me anymore."

"Move in with us."

"I'm sorry... what?"

"Your apartment or your room... whatever you want to call it. That can't be safe. Not with your roommates. The way they let me in? They'll do the same with the cop. And whatever he has planned for you will be worse. Plus it's more money you can set aside."

She ponders that information for a moment like it rings true for her.

"How do I know I'm safe with you three? Especially you?"

"I had you by surprise the other day. If I was going to do something, I would have done it."

"And Finn and Hudson?"

"You already know Finn. He'll hurt people but only the ones

who deserve it. And Hudson wouldn't hurt a fucking fly. Might irritate you by talking too fucking much, but not hurt you.

"I don't see us getting along very well." She looks me over. She's not wrong. We're both too headstrong and independent.

"We won't. But we need each other. That should be enough for the time being."

"This is insane..." she mutters, shaking her head and staring out the window.

"It's where we are."

"Okay. I guess... Okay."

"Get your shit packed. You move tomorrow. I'll send Finn to help."

"Tomorrow?"

"You want to wait and see if that cop shows up first or you want to get these paintings?"

She makes a face but nods her acquiescence.

"Good. Now I've gotta go back in before your coworker thinks I dined and dashed and calls the cops on me."

"I'll go in with you and explain. She won't call the cops. She was gushing over how hot you were."

"So I could make it up to her with a quick fuck break in my car?" I smirk. I don't mean it. I say it to see her reaction, and the flash of her green eyes over me as she throws open her door tells me all I need to know. Now I just have to hope I can handle her being under the same roof.

SEVEN

F inn

"She's moving in tomorrow," Rowan says as he puts the bags of takeout on the table for us.

"Who's moving in tomorrow?" Hudson asks as he grabs some forks from the drawer.

"The would-be damsel in distress with the gun fetish."

"Charlotte?" I ask, suddenly interested in this development.

"Yes, *Charlotte*." He says her full name like it's interesting and offensive all at the same time.

"The girl who wanted to shoot you is moving in with us?" Hudson's tone is incredulous.

"We need her, and it turns out she needs us."

"What do you mean she needs us?" I frown as I open some of the boxes and Hudson starts distributing the food on our plates.

"I went to check up on her today—"

"Stalk her, you mean," Hudson interrupts and smirks at me, knowing he'll rile Rowan.

"Do the research you claim you couldn't do." Rowan levels him with a look. "And she got attacked out in the parking lot by a fucking asshole cop."

"Attacked?" My heart sinks. Charlotte might have played the badass the other night but as long as I've known her, she's always been the sweet quiet one. The idea of her being attacked in a parking lot sends a chill down my spine and makes me want to beat someone's ass.

"Please don't tell me you got in a fight with a cop." Hudson frowns.

"No. He was gone by the time I got to her. But her story's a lot more complicated than I would have guessed." Rowan scoots a couple of beers across the table before he opens his own and grabs a piece of pie he brought back for himself out of the bag.

"Meaning?" I ask.

"She needs the money too. Owes the cop thanks to her brother and whatever he was involved in."

"Why is that not the brother's problem?" Hudson asks before he bites into his burger.

"It's her baby brother. I guess he's got problems of his own. Got in deep with the dirty cop and now he won't let her brother go until the debt's paid off."

"Fuck..." Hudson mumbles around the bite he's just taken and shakes his head.

"Yeah." Rowan's eyes flick to me. "You're awfully quiet about your fangirl."

I give him a sideways glance. "I didn't know anything about her circumstances. I told you—our interactions have been minimal."

"Right. Which is why the two of you were making fucking googly eyes at each other when she was threatening to kill me."

Hudson laughs before we both glare at him, stuffing another bite of his burger in his mouth as he looks away.

"Go get her and help her move tomorrow. Practice is canceled, so you should be free after class." Rowan looks back at me again.

"I thought you were the one fucking her. Why don't you help her?" I don't like the way he orders me around.

"When hate fucking her brains out is a solution, I'll happily fucking take care of it. When she needs emotional support and help moving heavy shit—that's where you come in. You can work on getting more information out of her. She only spilled shit to me today because she was rattled, and I was the lesser evil. She actually likes you."

"He has a point." Hudson shrugs, and we both glare at him again. He's literally incapable of keeping his mouth shut sometimes, and someday that is going to get him in trouble. In this house if not elsewhere.

"Fine. I'll check on her. For the record, I think this is a terrible idea. Where is she even going to sleep?"

"The couch." Rowan shrugs nonchalantly.

"The couch? She's not some dude crashing on the weekend, Rowan."

"She'll live. It's free and safer than where she is."

"Or we could treat her well instead of like she's a stray cat with mange we're reluctantly taking in," Hudson pipes in.

"I don't need your opinion, Mr. Fancy as Fuck. I need her in this house. She needs financial help and safety from the people who want to make her life miserable. She has it. I'm not fucking putting her up in a five-star hotel or rolling out the red carpet. Both of you can shut the fuck up about it and get on board, or we can have problems again."

"Fine," Hudson and I agree in unison but in very different tones.

"And to be clear—no one touches her." Rowan's eyes meet mine and there's a meaningful look in them. "No one."

"Not a problem," Hudson says dismissively.

I pause for a long beat, staring back at him. We don't fight over women. We almost came to blows once over one at the beginning of our friendship, and we agreed we'd never do it again. But I like Charlotte, more than I thought possible with each new thing

I learn about her. Having him tell me I don't have a chance to explore that? My gut tells me to argue. But my head tells me to get in line. That no woman is worth it. Besides, Rowan's interest in a woman never holds anyway. A couple of weeks and he's bored. With the way she irritates him, it might even be shorter than that. But I still don't like the way he throws down a gauntlet over it.

"Fine," I answer at last, letting the bitter tone come through on the word. Rowan studies me for a moment before he relents, turning his attention elsewhere.

"I'm gonna try to relax. Don't bother me unless it's an emergency." Rowan walks off, and I give him the middle finger once he's trudging up the stairs.

Eight

C harlotte

The next afternoon I'm packing up my stuff in the room I've rented for the last year, tossing things into my suitcase and a couple of boxes I took from the diner. I gave the landlords my thirty days' notice and my final payment which nearly wiped my bank account out.

But Rowan's right. I don't have a choice. I've told him too much. I know too much—we know too much about each other now. This stupid clusterfuck of fate has us both in a chokehold and moving in with him is the best shot I have of staying safe and getting the money I need.

I'll still have to work at the diner for the time being though. Even if we can pull off our planned heist and get top dollar for the paintings—an unlikely prospect—I still want to keep things looking like nothing's ever changed. Any sort of sudden deviation would make us all seem suspicious.

I'm deep in one of the bottom drawers of my dresser, packing the clothes I can never seem to find when I need them when a knock at the door startles me. I look up, and Finn's massive frame is filling the doorway. My heart flutters in my chest. The sweater he has on is tight around his shoulders and traps, making him look even bigger than usual, and when he sees me on my knees bent over the drawer he gives me a panty-dropping grin that takes the flutters up a notch to full-on palpitations.

"Rowan said you might need some help moving boxes. So I thought I'd come see."

"Can't help with boxes himself, can he?"

"Not really his thing, no. Getting his hands dirty, doing the tedious stuff—that's what he's got the rest of us for."

"You always do his dirty work?"

"Depends on what it is." He leans over to get a box off the floor for me and when he stands we're inches away from each other. His face is so close to mine that I could just close the small gap and kiss him. Close enough I can see the flecks of gold in his green eyes.

"Or who it is," I whisper.

His eyes drift to mine and then down to my lips. I swear he's about to kiss me when he pulls away suddenly, putting distance between us. I want to ask if I'm imagining things. If this is all in my head, but I don't want to make it awkward when I sincerely could use his help moving things today.

"Can't believe he talked you into this." He grabs another box and helps me put things inside, moving on like nothing happened.

"He's persuasive. But I imagine you know that since I never pictured you being a thief."

Finn's face shifts like he's considering that.

"Maybe you don't know me that well." He shrugs but then he smiles. "Although it seems like that goes both ways."

"Was definitely a weird way to meet outside of class."

"I just never see you at any of the parties or games."

"I'm busy most of the time. Too busy for fun."

"The professor's not fun?" He gives me a pretend look of shock and grasps his chest.

I roll my eyes in response and toss a few more things in the box. I know he's only playing. Despite being in league with Rowan and having a temper that gets him in a lot of fights, the Finn I've known in class has always been quiet and thoughtful.

"Don't judge me."

"I'm not. I assume you had your reasons." The smile turns into a more serious look.

"I honestly liked him at first. I guess I fell for the act when things first started. That I was special or whatever. Then I was in deep before I realized what was happening. The way he was manipulating and using me. Not that I can complain too much considering my plans for his paintings. Or I guess our plans now."

"I thought he was a good guy too. At least until he didn't pay us back. Then finding out the way he's been with you... He deserves whatever is coming his way. Probably more." I see the stormy look on Finn's face.

"Let's not do anything rash." I raise a brow at him.

"I'm not, I just... I don't know. Guys like that piss me off. Abuse of power pisses me off."

"You're kind of hard to read." I study him for a moment before I try to stop gawking at him and keep my focus on the task at hand.

He laughs. "You think so? I think you're the first person to say that."

"You're just so calm and collected most of the time. Kind of nerdy. But then the right thing sets you off..." I shrug. "And I know your reputation as an enforcer on the team. Hard to make sense of it sometimes."

"You don't like guys who fight, I'm guessing? If you found someone like the professor attractive at first, I'm going to guess the nerdy thing is what got you." He grabs the tape off the top of a dresser and starts working on the boxes that are full.

I glance down at him, trying to puzzle out if he's asking if I like him or if this is just a generic conversation on his part. Something about Finn has always made my stomach twist but being close to him like this, knowing I'm moving in with him even temporarily is making me hyper-aware of every little thing he does and says.

"I don't know. It can be hot under the right circumstances."

"You should come to a game sometime. If you haven't seen a fight on the ice yet, you're missing out." He smirks.

"I've always wanted to see you play." The words are out before I can stop them, and I turn my back to shield my face, worried I'm going to blush.

"Oh yeah?" I can hear the amusement in his voice.

"Yeah." I smile even though I'm trying not to.

We work like that for the rest of the afternoon—loading boxes, taping them, chatting about our predicament, and subtly flirting until everything is packed up. Moving in with these guys might not be the end of the world if it means I get to spend more time around Finn.

NINE

R owan

"So where's my room?" She looks at me.

"I told you I had a couch." I nod to the one in our living room where Hudson is currently sprawled out playing a video game.

"I thought you were kidding." Her brow furrows.

"You can have the couch in the den if you prefer. There's a pocket door but it's smaller and less comfortable. And you'll have to get out any time I need the room. I work in there."

"As opposed to the couch out here that's rarely used?" Her sarcasm seeps through and irritates me. I have sympathy for her, an inkling of it after seeing her in the car the other day, but she's already wearing on my nerves with her duchess act, and she's barely gotten in the door.

"Do you normally complain about free things when you get them?"

"This is far from free. You want me here because you want my help with the paintings."

"Paintings you need as much as we do."

"So what if I need to sleep because I have a shift at the diner and you're out here playing video games or having a party?"

"You have a car, right?" I don't mean it, not really, but I'm pissed she's asking stupid questions. I don't have the energy for stupid right now. "Take a nap in it."

"Are you fucking—"

"She can sleep in my bed. It's fine," Finn interjects, trying to keep the peace.

I watch the way her face lights up with that suggestion, and I hate it.

"The fuck she will. So the two of you can end up fucking and then she hates you when you need to kick her out of your bed for the next one? No fucking thank you. I don't need that drama. In fact, that's a house fucking rule. The two of you don't fuck." It was a good rule, even if it aligned with my self-interests.

I know Finn doesn't love it, but he also realizes I'm not entirely wrong.

"You don't tell me who I fuck."

"And you don't tell me where guests sleep in my house, Duchess. So bunk up." I point to the couch and see Hudson looking at me wide-eyed.

"Excuse me? Duchess?" She takes a step toward me like she might be up for violence.

"Entitled as fuck to come in here and start telling us what to do."

"I knew this was a mistake. I'm going to go back and see if I can get my old room back. There's no way I can live here." She snatches up her bags from the floor and storms toward the door, but Finn intercepts her before she gets too far.

"Just wait. We can make it work. I'm sure we can come to some compromises. Get you some privacy and make sure you get sleep when you need it. You don't need to run out yet. Let's figure it out, okay?"

"You honestly think he can be reasonable?" She gives him a look.

"I just want to see if we can make this work," Finn answers her calmly. I don't like the way he's always so quiet and calm around her either. The last thing I need is her making a gentleman out of him.

"Not as long as your friend is a fucking asshole." She glances back at me, and I give her a smarmy grin in return.

"That's unlikely to change," Finn says it like it's a matter of course, and it makes me laugh. A thing she doesn't like. The woman doesn't like anything about me. That combined with the fact she clearly wants to climb my best friend is grinding on my last fucking nerve along with her attitude.

I'm trying to remind myself I need her. That she's a critical piece of this puzzle, and somehow we'll have to figure out how to work together. But at the moment? I just want her to be as pissed off as I am. Like a fucking reverb—every bit of me that hurts for her. And now that she's here in my house, she's going to do what I want, when I want.

She turns around abruptly and looks back at me. A smile comes and goes before her eyes meet mine.

"I have your gun. You still want it back, right?" She softens the look on her face but her eyes dance with a taunt.

Fucking hell.

"What do you want?"

"A place to put my clothes and somewhere I can sleep with a proper door when I need to. Preferably not a couch."

Finn gives me a meaningful look over her shoulder. One that tells me to play along for the sake of peace.

"Fine." I practically growl the word. I start up the steps and turn back when she doesn't follow. "You coming?"

She reluctantly trails behind, and I imagine she's regretting her decision already. She was probably hoping Finn or Hudson would come to her rescue again. That I'd relent and let her and Finn start playing house. I open the door to my room and usher

her in. She stops just inside the threshold and looks around, turning back to look at me.

"Is this your room?"

"Yes. I have a big closet. I only use half of it, you can put your shit in there." I move toward it, opening the door and turning on the light. The place we live in is off campus, and I'm fairly certain it was owned by a family before this. My room, the master, is set up for a couple. There's a large his and hers closet. A bathroom with a shower made for two and a big soaking tub. It definitely wasn't designed for someone like me, and she's taking that in with interest.

"Okay... Thank you."

"Don't bother with the niceties. Where's the gun?"

"I don't have it with me, but I'll bring it to you."

"Tonight."

"Tomorrow."

"Tonight."

We stare at each other for a minute, but she relents from arguing.

"Fine. Where can I sleep when the couch isn't available?"

"Here." I point to my bed.

"So you can murder me in my sleep?"

"I need you until we finish this job. So until then, you can assume I won't murder you."

"Seems like a big assumption."

"Probably is. Especially when you run your fucking mouth."

"Why won't you just let me sleep in Finn's bed? Less inconvenient for you, and I'd feel safer."

"Oh, I'm sure you would feel safer." I laugh, and she narrows her eyes. "I told you why. I don't need you fucking my guys and clouding their heads. I don't need you getting attached 'cause one of them sticks his dick in you once and you decide you're in love."

She rolls her eyes. "That's ridiculous. So what then? You can fuck me, and it'll be fine?"

"You offering, Duchess?" I smirk.

"No."

"I don't have the same weaknesses they do. I don't feel bad for anyone—least of all you."

"Perfect. I don't need anyone's pity—least of all yours."

"Good. Put your shit away and then go get my gun." I turn and leave the room, too happy to put some distance between the two of us. Because despite what I say, the woman makes me want to fucking pin her against a wall and fuck her hard.

.

TEN

C harlotte

After going to the grocery store to pick up the ingredients they don't have, I come back to the house with what I need to make pasta, garlic bread, and salad for the four of us. In part to live up to the promise I made about cooking a couple of meals a week as rent, and in part to try to ingratiate myself with my hosts. Rowan is probably immovable on that front, but I still have hope that Finn and Hudson might come around to my side—especially Finn. And in addition to the fact that I genuinely like him, he'll be a good asset to have on my side against Rowan.

I check the time, seeing that I have about forty-five minutes left before they're done with practice, I send a text to Finn to let them know they don't have to pick up food on the way back. Then I set to work, buzzing around the kitchen. It's bare bones in here, barely a colander in sight, but it's enough to make do.

By the time they get home, I'm getting dinner on the table, and the fresh garlic bread is coming out of the oven that I'm fairly certain hasn't seen anything but a frozen pizza as long as they've lived here.

"Holy shit! It smells good in here. What are you making, Charlotte?" Hudson asks, tossing his bags down near the door as Rowan and Finn follow him in and do the same.

"Pasta and garlic bread. Thought we could all have dinner together." I glance up at them with a smile as I go to drain the pasta in the sink.

"Surprised you know how to cook," Rowan quips right before Finn elbows him in the side, frowning at him.

"Thank you. It smells amazing. Just give me a second, and I'll set the table," Finn offers.

"That would be great. Thanks." I flash a smile at him, ignoring Rowan before I return to my task.

"I can help too. Just let me change," Hudson volunteers. I nod and smile as they both run upstairs.

Rowan keeps quiet and wanders into the kitchen, grabbing a piece of the garlic bread and taking a bite. His eyes light and one brow raises.

"Not bad."

"I work at a diner. The cooks have taught me a thing or two."

"Trying to win them over with a family dinner?"

"Maybe. Mostly just trying to work toward some sort of peace. We're all going to have to get along, right?"

He shrugs. "As long as we don't fuck each other over, I don't know that we have to get along."

"Doesn't that require trust?" I glance back over my shoulder as I start getting the final things ready for the meal.

"Trust is complicated. The only rule is no lies in the house. We all tell each other the truth, then we don't have to worry about trust."

We stare at each other for a moment as I ponder that thought, only breaking the connection when Finn and Hudson reenter the room and start the chaos of rooting through the cabinets to pull out dishes.

"By the way, we need to get more paper plates and cups for the party." Hudson looks to Rowan as he pulls salt and pepper out of the pantry.

"What party?" I ask because no one has mentioned it to me. I imagine it means I'm going to lose my couch if they're hosting it here.

"Saturnalian party this weekend." Hudson grins.

"More like Bacchanalian party." Finn laughs as he starts putting plates down on the dining table.

"Saturnalian party?" I repeat, looking to Rowan who ignores me, instead nibbling away at his garlic bread and going to the fridge for a beer.

"We have one every year. Kind of like St. Nick's Day. But wilder and uh... more intimate." Hudson has an amused look on his face.

"Intimate and wild sounds like my couch is going to get defiled."

"Oh, it definitely is, Duchess." Rowan smirks.

"So where am I supposed to sleep?"

"There isn't much sleeping." Finn flashes me a look from over the table that makes my stomach twist.

"Rowan is usually Lord of Misrule and decides the night's events. But sex, drugs, and drinking are always at the top of the list," Hudson informs me.

"Lord of Misrule?" I look back to Rowan again.

"Master of Ceremonies... Creator of Chaos..." Hudson laughs again, and I can tell this is one of their favorite things. "We all wear our masks. You can put your name in a bowl to get a mystery partner for the night. Lots of wine and old-style feast foods—cakes, fruit, liquors. We go all out for it."

"It's invite-only but everyone tries to get an invite on campus. How have you not heard of this before?" Finn raises a brow.

"Sounds interesting. I've never cared much for wild parties," I mumble as I carry things to the table. Mostly because they end up with me in a closet with Rowan, enjoying myself until the hangover the next morning.

"You'll like this one. Stick with me, and you'll have a good time." Hudson grins and bumps my shoulder, and I smile back as we sit down to dinner.

"Okay, but when are we going to plan our…" I start and then I realize I don't even know what to call it. Robbery sounds pretty terrible even if that's what it is. Is there a word for justified robbery? Vengeance acquisition? Punishment pilfering?

"Heist?" Finn adds helpfully.

"Sure. Heist." That at least sounds more like we're professionals with a common goal than the petty thieves we actually are.

"We gotta get through our game this weekend and then the party. After all that we can formulate a plan for getting the paintings. I'm thinking Christmas weekend though. Hopefully the professor goes out of town." Rowan takes a bite of his pasta, and his brows raise subtly like he might like it as much as the garlic bread. Maybe the man can be mildly impressed.

"Fine. As long as it's soon. I want to get this done." I take a sip of my ice water and glance to make sure Finn and Hudson are enjoying their food too, and my heart bounces a little when I see them both devouring their dinner. I suppose it doesn't take much to keep hockey players happy with food after practice, but it still feels like a small win.

Eleven

Fⁱⁿⁿ

When we get off the ice that night after the game I'm exhausted and bloody. The shower in the locker room isn't nearly enough to knock the weariness from my body. I'm going to need a soak when I get home to try to ease my muscles and take the sting off the worst of the bruises from the fight tonight. When we get to the car, Charlotte's standing there, and she pops off the side of it when she sees us coming. I grin at the way she hurries toward me, concern written on her face.

"Are you okay? That fight was insane." She frowns as she looks me over, and I hear Rowan make a scoffing sound.

"I'm fine. Just need an Epsom soak and some ice. I'll be good as new tomorrow. You like watching the fight?"

"I doubt that. And it was interesting..." Her fingers ghost over the bruise on my cheek once we're in the car—Rowan driving, Hudson in the passenger seat, and the two of us in the back. I see Rowan's eyes flash a warning look at me in the rearview at the way she's touching me and given the rough night and my ejection from the game, I'm half tempted to argue. Half tempted to tell him if she wants to take care of me tonight, I'll let her.

But as I sit back against the seat and glance out the window, I remember that he's kept us afloat. Kept me out of trouble more than once over the years even when it meant him taking the fall. I can't betray all those years for her even if I want to. Even if I'm so fucking tempted it hurts.

We stop on the way back, grabbing some quick food for all of us, and I take my soak after we eat. When I get out, she's waiting in my room with ice packs, I start to smile, but when I look closely I see her cheeks are stained and her eyes are red.

"Charlotte? Are you okay?" My voice startles her, and she looks up.

"What? Oh yeah. I'm okay. I just wanted to make sure you had some ice and stuff. Those bruises look terrible."

"Why were you crying? Did Rowan do something?" I feel my temper start to kick at the idea of him being an ass to her again for no reason.

"Rowan? No. No. I just... The guy that has my brother. He sent a video of him telling me he's okay and not to worry. But that asshole told me to hurry the fuck up with his money. Like I can go any faster. He knows I've done all I can. I'm just worried if we don't get the money in time. What will happen?"

"Oh fuck." I sit next to her on the bed and wrap an arm around her shoulders. She leans into me, the warmth of her body soaking into mine.

"I'm just scared for him. Before he'd let me talk to Brady occasionally, but now, he won't even do that. Just the videos. I mean he looks okay, considering. He tells me not to worry. But he's basically being held for ransom while I try to work off his debt. How the hell am I supposed to not worry?" A little sob comes out then, and her tears start to fall again.

"We're gonna figure it out. We'll get the paintings and get the money soon." I pull her closer. I wish I could fix this for her. Beat this guy into a fucking pulp for what he's doing to her and her brother.

Rowan chooses that moment to walk by my open door, and he pulls up short when he sees the two of us sitting on my bed while I try to console her. His face contorts though when he sees the tears, and he leans against the doorframe.

"What's wrong?"

Charlotte starts at the sound of his voice, her head popping up, and her eyes snapping to his immediately. It's hard to tell if it's fear or something else when she's around him.

"Nothing. It's fine."

"It's obviously not." His jaw tightens, annoyed that she's sharing her problems with me and dismissing him outright.

"Her brother. The cop's threatening again and hassling her about the money." I play peacemaker.

"Desperate men make threats. If he wanted to hurt him, he would have done it." Rowan says flatly, his eyes skimming over her and landing hard on the spot where our bodies meet.

"I don't trust him not to hurt him. I just want him back."

"We're working on it. You just have to be patient."

"Like you'd be patient if it was your brother they were torturing."

I tense a little, waiting for Rowan's reaction. His brother wasn't tortured exactly, but he saw horrific things happen to him before he died. Too much of his life was spent trying to run the same kind of games Rowan does and getting caught by the wrong sorts of people. Things we shouldn't have had to see when we were kids. Things his mother should have protected them from if she hadn't left him behind with his ailing grandparents for, what I can only assume she thought was, a better life without them.

"You're right. I wouldn't be. But if we aren't patient, and we make stupid mistakes because we're in a hurry, we won't be able to get the paintings or the money."

"I know. I just... wish this could all move faster." She swipes at the tears on her cheek.

"When the professor's gone, we'll take them. The cop gave you six more weeks when you gave him the last payment, right?" Rowan almost gives her a look of sympathy, and now I know there's something more there than he wants to admit.

"Yes, but we have to sell them in that time too."

"We'll figure it out. Between the four of us, we've got this," I say to reassure her.

"And if we don't?" She looks to Rowan because, I think as much as she wants to believe me, she still isn't sure if she should believe him.

"We'll make it happen." Rowan's eyes darken and his jaw sets. She might have her misgivings, but I don't. Because I know him, and at this point, I think he'd do anything to make it happen just to prove to her he could.

TWELVE

udson

The Saturnalian party has been raging all night, and I've made a spot for myself up on the staircase where I can watch the festivities without getting lost in them. Charlotte comes up and settles next to me on the stairs, watching the madness of the party unfold below. I shove my mask back on my head. The thing is fucking making me sweat in a house that's already overfilled and overheated, and I can't stand having it on for more than a few minutes at a time. The more I drink, the shorter that time gets.

Her fingers brush over my cheek, and I look over at her. A drunken smile plays at her lips, accentuating the cupid's bow that's already tempting as fuck to kiss. Which I can't. Because I've got a fucking girl—one who won't answer my texts but is still technically mine, and Rowan and Finn are already about to come to blows over her. Even if I was single, adding myself into that mix is a recipe for fucking disaster.

"You have pretty cheekbones," she muses, as her fingers—cold from the drink in her hand—drift their way down my jaw and over my chin. "And this cleft. Gives you character. It's hot."

I smirk at her, amused at her honesty, and touched that she feels comfortable talking to me like this. We've settled into an easy friendship—hanging out on the couch watching TV together, having me explain hockey to her, and her occasionally beating my score playing my latest video game. Whatever her attraction is to Rowan and Finn, she wouldn't talk to them like this—be so honest and cavalier with her thoughts. And I'll take it, happily.

"Now I'm gonna have to journal about that, Duchess."

Her smile falters. "Duchess? Really? It's bad enough that they call me that. I can take care of myself."

"Rowan never quite grew out of the schoolyard teasing. He does it because he likes you."

"I bet." She rolls her eyes. "And what's your excuse?" Her eyes narrow on me.

"I like the idea of you as a Duchess." I lift my eyebrow and smirk at her.

"Yeah. I don't think I could fill those shoes. Too damned to be proper like that." She tilts her drink forward shaking her head before she takes a sip.

She might not be wrong, and I'm fairly certain she's dragging us all down with her. I watch as her eyes float to Finn. He's on the couch with two girls draped over him, but he's distracted, looking at his phone before his eyes search the room like he's looking for something—someone. I glance back at Charlotte, and she's staring down at her cup like the patterns in the ice might have answers for her.

"I just want to go to bed, which I can't do. Unless I go to Rowan's, and we all know I'll probably be woken up by whatever woman he's fucking tonight." She glances up to frown at the couch, her eyes stuttering over the spot where Finn's fingers play with the strap of the brunette's dress.

"You can sleep in my bed," I offer without thinking about how it will sound.

Her eyes snap to mine and her brow knits in confusion.

"Not like that. Girlfriend and all. Just mean it's empty right now, and no one will go in there. I'm obviously not taking anyone back to fuck in it. I can wake you up when I go to bed. It'll probably be when the party's over, and your couch is free again."

A small smile flickers over her face once more, and she leans her head against my shoulder.

"You're the one bright spot in this place, you know. You have a good heart. I don't know why you run around with them."

"They've been good friends to me."

"I guess if you're something more than a paycheck to them, it's possible."

"You're more than a paycheck to them."

She scoffs.

"You are. They're just fucking pacing around each other trying not to piss the other one off."

"Meaning what?" She frowns, not following my meaning.

"They both want to fuck you. But the whole blood is thicker than water thing."

Another frown. "They're not actual brothers."

"The saying's misinterpreted. The original saying was that the blood that was shed was thicker than the water of the womb. So forged bonds are closer than familial ones." I'm rambling. I have no idea why I'm telling her this like a fucking weirdo. I talk too damn much for my own good, and it's a particular problem around her.

"Huh." Her brow unknits, and she takes another sip of her watered-down drink, shaking the ice to get the last of it. "I didn't know that."

"Yeah... And those two have been through a lot together. Don't let anything come between them."

"It's not that serious. I just... had a minor crush on Finn, I guess. You know that person who's always in your classes, but you never talk with them. But they're always there, and you have this parasocial thing going because you're both always occupying the same space and—"

She stops when she sees me raise my eyebrow. Apparently, she's as weird and rambling as I am. At least when she's had a little to drink.

"A minor crush, eh?"

"I'm over it."

"You're not over it."

"I don't think I have a choice." She looks at Finn again as one of the girls whispers something in his ear, and he gives her a half smile.

I know him well enough to know he's not interested, and I've watched him scan the room enough times to know that he's either worried about where Rowan is or worried about where she is. More than likely it's both.

She sighs. "All right. Well if you're serious, I'm taking you up on that offer."

"I'm serious. Go get some sleep." I run my hand over the top of her head, scruffing it like she's a little kid, and she rolls her eyes.

"You gonna stay out here and watch everyone else get paired up to fuck?" Her eyes flick to the glass bowl Rowan's got out. The one where everyone's dumped their names for some chaotic fun.

"Yeah. Might have some amusing results."

She shakes her head again and runs her fingers over my shoulder, leaving goosebumps in their wake that she thankfully can't see through my shirt.

"Getting some water and then off to bed. Goodnight, Hudson."

"Night, Duchess."

Her eyes narrow, but she smiles before she takes off down the stairs.

Thirteen

C harlotte

I walk into the den after I get my water, sliding back the pocket door behind me to keep the chaos of the party out but not fully shutting it. I should go to bed, but I'm nosy. Still wanting to watch this scene with Finn play out.

This way I can sit on the old leather couch and watch without having to be a part of it. With this current angle, I also get a good view of him posted up on the couch surrounded by a small fan base gushing over the way he played tonight—men and women alike.

I lean against the pocket door and take a sip of the water I should be chugging, peering at him through the slit in the doors. The cut under his eye is still fresh and red, his hair still a little damp, and the mask—he and the guys are still wearing them like it's their new favorite thing—lays on the back of the couch behind him.

There's a fangirl on either side of him, a brunette and another girl with blonde hair that fades into pink, and they're both running their hands all over him. He looks at one with the occasional smile when she says something, and then changes his attention to the other, only pausing to answer questions about hockey. He'll probably end up in bed with both of them tonight while I lay on the couch listening. Moving into this house has been a mistake. Even if I am less likely to get hurt by Steven here.

Suddenly there's breath against my neck and over the back of my ear, an arm stretches out over my shoulder caging me against the door, and I hear an amused low raspy chuckle. My heart comes to a brief stop in my chest before it restarts, faster than before. I *hate* the effect he has on me.

"He never has found a threesome he didn't like," Rowan muses, his warm body brushing over mine from behind as he follows my line of sight. "Gonna be a disappointing night for you, Duchess."

"Don't you have better things to do? Misruling or whatever it is you're the lord of tonight?"

"I needed a break."

I've noticed that about Rowan. That sometimes it seems like all the crowds and chaos are too much for him, even at his games, and he retreats from it as quickly as he can. That some of his showmanship is false bravado. Not that he'd ever admit it.

The scent of berries wafts through the air, and I turn around to look up at him. His lashes sheltering his thoughts as he studies me.

"Are you wearing fruity cologne? Or did you just get mauled by a girl wearing a lot of it?" My lips quiver with amusement.

His brow furrows, and he holds up his hand, a blackberry between his thumb and forefinger before he pops it in his mouth, giving me a stormy look.

"That's... a weird snack." I raise a brow.

"They're my favorite. Didn't get a lot of fresh fruit at the one shitty grocery we had on our side of town, and if we did it was mostly rotten."

"Fair." I'd really only gotten the good kind that wasn't old and half-rotten when we visited my grandmother. She had a huge garden and a small, forested area on her property where there were lots of wild berries. We'd lay in the grass and eat them while staring up at the sky trying to make sense of the shapes in the clouds.

He takes one and presses it to my lips, and I part them. He pushes it in with his thumb, and I crush down on the plump piece of fruit with my teeth. The sweet flavor rushing over my tongue as he puts another in his mouth. His eyes drift over my face, and his hand comes back to my chin, sliding underneath it as his thumb swipes over the corner of my lip.

There's an intent look on his face like he's remembering something, and I wonder if maybe he had the same kind of child-hood memories I did. I wonder what little Rowan would have looked like. An innocent version of this man is hard to imagine.

"What?" I ask softly.

"Just thinking about what you'd look like spread out on a table covered in them. Drizzling blackberry liquor over these gorgeous tits." His finger slides down in between the low vee of my shirt, his eyes following it.

It's the last thing I expected him to say, though I should be used to it. It's always something crass with him. Tender bonding moments are not his strong suit.

"Now you sound like Mitch."

"He likes to drink that expensive whiskey collection of his off them?"

"He was more into toes than tits."

"Was he?" His eyes light with mischief, and I immediately regret giving him any morsel of information. "That'll be useful."

"Useful for inspiring you?" I counter, trying to distract him from whatever scheming he's doing as if it's possible to redirect Rowan when he's focused.

"Going to use it on the long list of things we do to bend him."

"That's cruel. You want your fetishes used against you?"

"Always." A wry smile crosses his lips.

I roll my eyes, turning around to glimpse the party again and see that one of Finn's companions has made her way into his lap. My gut churns at the sight of it, and I close my eyes. I need to go upstairs and go to bed like I told Hudson I would.

"You don't like yours used against you?" Rowan wraps an arm around my waist and pulls me flush against his body, resting his head against mine, his lips a few inches from my ear. "Like the fact you like to watch him all the time. Wishing it was you in his lap. Don't you?"

Rowan's other hand drifts up my side and over my chest, slipping under the top and bustier I have on. He cups my breast, and his thumb plays over my nipple. I don't move to stop him, giving him silent permission. I hate the man, but I love the way his hands feel on me. The way he looks when he touches me.

"Or would you rather be on your knees for him? I bet you'd love sucking his cock, wouldn't you? Taking him deep down your throat until you choke on him. Knowing you're all he sees." His lips brush over the side of my neck, and I lean against the pocket door, watching Finn and wishing it was him touching me like this. "You want that, don't you?" Rowan presses.

"Yes." It's the truth, one he already knows, but he punishes me for it, pinching my nipple and grazing his teeth over my neck. "Fuck, Rowan."

His hands drift down, and he starts undoing the button on my pants, his fingers on the zipper a moment later, the sound of it so loud in this room despite the din of the party just beyond the door. He hesitates though, just as his fingertips hit the edge of my underwear.

"Tell me to stop. Tell me you fucking hate me and don't want my hands on you." His words are low, and the raspy nature of his voice does something for me even though I wish it didn't. I'm surprised he asks at all, but then I'm fairly certain the question is more about his ego than anything else—him wanting to know that it's not just Finn I'm imagining.

"I hate you." It's the best I can do because we all swore no lies in this house.

He grins against my skin before he slips his fingers under the elastic, sliding two of them deep inside me as he kisses my shoulder, a soft vibration along my collarbone when he groans at how wet I am.

"Want it that fucking bad? Just thinking about it gets you this wet," he mutters the words as he kisses a trail up my neck. His fingers start to move inside me, and his palm grazes over my clit. I lean forward seeking more friction than I'm getting, and an amused rumble comes out of his chest.

"Fuck, you're so needy. So desperate for it."

"Whatever your ego needs to believe." I shouldn't taunt him, but I can't help myself. The desire to have him touch me almost as much as the desire to be able to cut as sharply as he does with his words.

He pulls away abruptly then, and I nearly fall into the door when he lets me go, catching myself just in time. I turn around and see him leaning back against the desk again. He pulls another couple of blackberries out of the bowl, his fingers still wet with me, and pops them in his mouth. His jaw works as his eyes rake over me, annoyance dancing across his face. I go to straighten my top and the bustier, to put myself back to rights.

"Don't." He glares at me. "In fact, fucking take that off."

"Why should I?"

"I can get you things you want, or I can take them away for good." He raises one shoulder in a half-shrug. "It's up to you."

I stare at him for a long minute, but then my hands go to the hem of the shirt and pull it over my head. I toss it onto the desk next to him like a challenge, and he glances at it and then at me, watching as I reach to undo the bustier next.

"Wait." Another berry goes into his mouth, tucked against his cheek before he speaks. "Oh fuck. Hudson would love that. Did you let him see?"

"Hudson has a girlfriend." I'd happily show him if it wasn't for the fact he's off-limits. They all should be, really. Apparently though, psychotic and disinterested aren't enough to dissuade me.

"Does he remember that?" Rowan muses more to himself than anyone. "Take it off." He doesn't bother to look up. Apparently, lingerie doesn't interest him. I'm not sure much does. He's the kind who would yawn during hardcore porn.

"You could ask nicely." I smile at him, my eyes letting him know how often I wish he'd die on the spot.

He grabs another handful of berries and crosses the space between us in a few short steps.

"Please let me see your fucking tits." His tone is crisp but not quite cruel. I raise my eyes to his, holding them while I undo the line of hooks and eyes at the back before I let it fall to the ground.

A sound of appreciation leaves him as his eyes drift over me, his hand coming forward to cup one breast, and his thumb teases my nipple as it starts to peak under his touch. He's soft, gentle even, in the way he touches me.

He crushes one of the berries between his fingers before he eats it, taking the juice left in its wake and smearing it over my nipple. A stain's left there before he leans down to run his tongue over it. I gasp at how warm his mouth is and the clever way his tongue circles the tip. He smirks when he releases me, musing at his handiwork while he pops the last berry in his mouth. He leans forward, grabbing me by the chin.

"Open." He gives my jaw a gentle squeeze, and I listen to him, parting my lips before he closes the distance and bites down on the berry, sliding it into my mouth with his tongue, some of the juice dribbling over my lip and down my chin.

"Good, isn't it?" He pulls back to study my face.

"I prefer raspberries."

"I bet you fucking do."

He kisses me roughly then, grabbing me by the throat and pinning me up against the door. My head hits the wood, and his body's so close to mine that I can feel how hard he is. I kiss him back and reach for the button on his pants. His hand tightens around my throat though and he pulls away from me.

"No. First, we get you what you want so badly. When you take my cock, I want you to be able to appreciate the difference."

I frown, trying to figure out what he means. But I don't have to wait long. A moment later he slides the pocket door open next to me, still shielding me from general view.

"Finn."

The way he says his name—it's a command. A summons. One Finn follows because a moment later he's in the room with us, a confused expression on his face until his eyes follow Rowan's to me. They rake over my naked and disheveled state, landing on my breasts and then falling down to where my pants and underwear are half-bunched around my hips before they cloud with lust. Finn slams the pocket door shut behind him, flipping the lock a second later and the sound of it ricochets in my chest and lands low.

Fourteen

F inn

Rowan's lip curls in recognition when he sees my face. He knows I want her. That I've stayed away because I know he wants her just as much, and my loyalty still outstretches my lust. He pulls her forward by the throat, placing her between us but wrapping an arm around her and splaying his hand over her abdomen.

"Should feel how wet she is. She's been in here fantasizing about sucking your cock."

Her eyes dart away, and her cheeks color. Charlotte isn't exactly shy, least of all around Rowan. But around me she's different—all lowered lashes and surreptitious smiles—things I eat up like I'm fucking starved when it comes to her.

"That true?" I reach for her, running my fingers along her jaw, trying to bring her back to me. Get her to look at me and let her know that I'm here for her now. That I'll make sure she gets rewards for her torment.

"Maybe," she whispers, something soft in her eyes when they finally meet mine.

"Maybe." Rowan laughs. "She thinks you're going to fuck those girls you had in your lap but won't do anything to stop it. So I thought I'd give her a little nudge."

I raise my brow at Rowan subtly. We've been dancing around the subject of her. He's made it clear he's laid a claim, one we all need to fall in line on. I just want to be sure this is him actually stepping out of the way and not just tormenting us for fun as part of his chaos act tonight.

"Is that what this is?" I glance down at her state of undress.

"Nah. This was for me. Wasn't it?" He kisses the side of her throat, and she closes her eyes, the slightest flutter of her lashes at his touch.

I tamp down hard on the jealousy I feel in its wake. That small sign that she wants him too. The kind of want that must be strong because these two hate each other most hours of the day. A barely stitched-together peace treaty that keeps us all on the same side.

One I worry will be ripped to shreds when one of them pushes the other too hard in a direction they don't want to go. It's why I don't completely hate the idea of them fucking. This desperate sort of pent-up desire they have between them is the only glue that might keep it all on track. But I want her too.

I swipe my thumb over the stain on her lower lip, brushing back and forth over the soft plump flesh there. I want her lips wrapped around my cock, want to feel how much she wants me. Knowing how good her plush lips are going to feel when she sucks me dry. I need it.

"Feel how wet she is," Rowan's voice is low, and when our eyes lock, I see the flicker of jealousy there. He's not used to this. Women come easily to him. Even more so than me.

My eyes shift to hers, searching for permission there as I reach to pull the rest of her clothes down.

"Are you wet for us?" I ask.

"Yes."

I push her pants and underwear down her legs, and she steps out of them, her gorgeous body on full display. A sight I've been dying for—one Rowan's taunted me about one too many times out on the ice.

"You want me to touch you?"

"Yes... Please." Her eyes meet mine with a look that might bring me to my knees.

There's a scoffing sound that comes from Rowan's throat. He hates how sweet she always is with me and Hudson. But he holds his tongue, his eyes flashing with irritation that dissipates a moment later when she leans her head back on his shoulder as I slip my fingers between her legs.

"Fuck me," I curse as she coats my fingers immediately.

"Warmed her up for you. Told her how good your cock would feel on her tongue. Didn't I?" His hands run over her body and goosebumps break out over her skin where he touches her.

"Y-yes," she stutters as I brush the pad of my thumb over her, circling her swollen clit. Her palms find my chest and run down it, landing on my belt and she starts to undo it. I'm hard as fuck, dying to feel her hands on me.

"You want to suck his cock?" Rowan asks, his eyes on me as he does it. Reminding me he's in charge. She nods her yes.

"Come here where you're comfortable then." He walks them back, sitting down on the Chesterfield leather couch, and pulls her into his lap.

She looks up at me then, her eyes bright with want, and she runs her tongue over her lower lip as she waits for me. I follow them over, undoing my belt and pants. I pull myself out and give my cock a stroke to take the edge off. The way she's looking at me, how perfect her body is—it's already too fucking good for me to take. A moment later though when her eyes land on my cock, going wide at my size, I can't help the grin that comes to my face.

I shouldn't gloat. It won't help when it comes to his temper. But it helps my ego, and knowing he's touched her first, made her come years ago before I could—at least I have this. Her desperate to take me down even when she's in his lap.

Her hand wraps around me, and her tongue darts out, sliding down the underside of my cock as her hand slips over me. A low moan comes out of me, and her eyes lift to my face.

"That's a good girl. Look at me. I want to see your eyes when you suck me." I brush a bit of hair out of her face and then thread my fingers through the violet strands when she takes me in her mouth. She's tentative at first, sucking on the tip and letting her hand do most of the work, nervously taking more of me with each pass.

"Take all of me, Charlotte. I know you can."

She takes me deeper then, letting me bump the back of her throat as she sucks and licks my cock. She's messy when she does it, moaning softly and generous with every touch and taste she takes. I slip my hand around the back of her head, tightening my grip in her hair.

"Let me help?" I meet her eyes, and she closes them in acknowledgment. I grip her hair and pull her closer and push her back, fucking her face slowly as she works the base of my cock with her hand.

My eyes shift to Rowan, checking in to make sure he's not losing his mind over how much she's enjoying this. But his hands are all over her, and he's kissing a trail down her spine as she writhes in his lap. I can see how desperate she is to be touched but he withholds it from her, teasing her with his hands up her inner thigh and then bypassing her clit to grip her hips instead.

"You need to be touched, don't you? So wet and desperate to come." I look down at her, and her eyes open again, acknowledging the damage we're doing to her composure and the fact that he won't touch her with a soft moan around my cock.

I look at him, and his eyes are open now, he looks up at me. I expect to see more anger there that I've inserted myself where he doesn't want me but there's none. Just lust and something like reverence while he watches her. She grinds back on him as she moves and his eyes shutter, hands going to her hips to pull her down on him. She must feel how hard he is because she moans again, and the vibrations take me so close to the edge that I'm the one who's desperate now.

Fifteen

C harlotte

I'm overwhelmed by the feeling of power at having both of them like this—Rowan hard beneath me while I writhe over his lap, and Finn so perfectly thick and hard in my mouth. My whole body is on fire, and Rowan's hands are everywhere all at once: down my sides, over my breasts, teasing his fingers over my inner thighs as he kisses and licks his way down my spine. I'm just greedy enough to want more—to have them both come for me.

I can tell Rowan wants his own turn. The way he's holding back. How quiet he is letting Finn play the good guy.

"So close," Finn mutters, his eyes shuttering, and I pick up my pace. I suck, lick, and moan my way over his cock until he's gripping my hair tight and fucking my mouth closer to his release. He starts to pull back, and I look up at him, pleading with my eyes to let me have all of him, and he relents. The warmth of him breaks over my tongue, and I swallow him down as fast as I can, turned on even more by the way he watches me.

"Fuck, you're good at that, Charlotte. So good for me." He finishes off, his eyes so soft and adoring that I melt a little under his gaze. His fingers brush over my lips and he gently cups my chin.

Rowan brings me back to reality when his fingers brush over my clit, and I realize how needy I am to have my own release.

"Fuck that was hot. She's soaked through my pants," Rowan mutters.

"She deserves to come after that. So fucking perfect," Finn's voice is raspier than normal, like some of it's been stolen away from him, and he runs his fingers under my chin one last time before he collapses next to Rowan on the couch.

"That true? You think you deserve to come?" Rowan asks me as his fingertips tease me again.

"No, but I want to," I answer. I slip out of his grasp for a moment, turning around and facing him. I'm not prepared for the look on his face. All the irritation and taunting that's usually there is gone, replaced by lust. The pure unadulterated kind that almost looks like adoration. My heart stutters in response to it.

"We both could," I whisper, leaning forward to brush my lips over his. I expect coldness in response, but he kisses me back with a rough sort of intensity that has me wanting more.

I want *this* Rowan. The one who's cracked open, a glimmer of the man I hope is somewhere inside. I reach for his pants, making quick work of the button and zipper there, pulling him out. I run my hand over him. He's almost as big as Finn, probably longer but not quite as thick. But he still feels perfect in my hands as I stroke him again, and he closes his eyes, pulling his lower lip between his teeth.

"Put me inside," he groans the command.

I hesitate, and he senses it. His eyes open and his eyebrow raises in question and then falls again.

"He just came down your throat and you didn't wonder."

"He doesn't hate me."

"I'm good, and I assume the professor means birth control and condoms."

I nod.

"Then take me so your cunt can know what a real cock feels like."

The words melt what little resistance I have left. I take his cock until he fills me, and I have to take a moment to adjust to his size. Mitch was the only sex I've had in recent history. Too busy for anything else. He'd been adequate—good enough to get the job done and nothing to complain about, at least before I knew what he really was.

But Rowan and Finn are in a different league than him—not just in this area, but all of them. One I might not belong in no matter how much I might want it. But for now, I get a taste, and I'll take it while I can.

"Fuck..." It's a low groan out of his chest when I start to move. He runs his hands over my hips as I ride him. His lids drop, and his head falls back on the couch as I start to take him deeper and faster.

I can feel Finn's eyes on me. Watching my expressions, the way my breasts sway with my movement, and then down to where I slide over Rowan's cock. Finn watches for a moment before he reaches out, his thumb positioned to massage my clit with each up-and-down motion of my body. I'm moaning from how good it is, and Rowan's eyes open again to watch.

"You like that? The way he touches you when you ride me?" Rowan's smirk resurfaces.

"I love it."

"Good. We're going to ruin you. Until we're the only ones you see." He grabs me and starts to counter my strokes, fucking me and using me how he wants even from beneath me. His arms and shoulders flex as he presses on my hips, and I'm distracted by the motion, wishing I had him as naked as I am. Finn starts to circle his thumb and the relentless assault from both of them has me on the brink, gasping and cursing with alternating effort as I feel the edge of my orgasm build.

"Come hard on my cock. Take me with you and show Finn how good it's gonna feel when you fuck him with this sweet little cunt. So fucking tight and perfect." His fingers bite into my hips as I start to fall over the edge of my release, begging for more of both of them and using Rowan's shoulders to keep myself upright.

He comes with a low groan a moment later, his hips slowing as I do, taking him in shallower passes as he curses about how good I feel. I collapse against his chest without thinking about it. Forgetting for a moment that I'm dealing with Rowan and not a man with feelings. I start to pull away, but he catches me, his mouth passing over my throat in slow absent strokes, his tongue teasing against the pulse beneath my ear before he grips me tight and whispers against it.

"You're ours now. The professor doesn't touch you. No one touches you who isn't me or Finn, you hear me?"

I swallow against the dryness in my mouth, surprised when the order warms every inch of me instead of making me want to rip his throat out. I nod, accepting my fate.

Sixteen

R owan

She agrees without protest, shocking me as I thought for sure there'd be an argument. But instead, her eyes just drift over my face, her brow knitting momentarily before it clears again. Like she's trying to work something out. But she doesn't say a word.

She pulls from my arms a moment later, and for that moment I worry she's going to go to Finn for comfort. But she surprises me by standing, grabbing tissues off the bookcase and her clothes, and slipping off to the corner to clean up and get dressed again. I do the same, pulling myself back together despite the fact she's made it difficult for me.

Finn watches her with rapt attention, and I know he's going to want her as often as he can have her now that I've dropped my demands where he's concerned. I'm too fucking tired of seeing the two of them watch each other like sad little lost souls to stop it anymore.

It's strategic on my part anyway. She's never going to love me.

She sees through too much of my mask to what's underneath. But she might end up falling in love with him, and I need her loyalty as much as I need to hear her gasping over my cock again.

She starts to walk out of the room but stops to look back at me.

"I was headed to bed. Hudson offered me his since the couch is obviously occupied. Is that a problem?"

Possibly, depending on what the fuck game Hudson is playing now.

"Yes," I answer immediately. "Mine or Finn's."

"Can I use your shower?"

"Yes." Now I have the sudden desire to watch her clean me off her body in my shower, but I can't. I have to go back to overseeing this debaucherous gathering. One I've already been absent from for too long. One I hope Hudson is overseeing with us gone. Maybe I can find him and find out where his head's at when it comes to her.

"Thank you," she says softly before she unlatches the pocket door and disappears out of it.

"Fuck me..." Finn scrubs a hand over his face.

"Yeah? Think maybe you can clear your fucking head now that you've got that out of the way?"

"Gonna need to clear it every fucking day." He grins stupidly.

"Just don't forget she belongs to both of us," I warn, already feeling a swell of bitter jealousy knowing she's probably running upstairs to recount how good he tasted.

"Unless Hudson tries to take her. We'll both lose out then." He laughs.

"Funny. But seriously, what the fuck is that about?"

"I'm sure it was innocent. He's so caught up on Sophia I don't think anyone else even registers for him." Finn dismisses it out of hand.

"Oh she fucking registers for him." I've seen the way Hudson looks at her.

Finn's smile flatlines, and he shakes his head, staring up at the ceiling. He never likes to say anything ill of Hudson. He's the good one of the three of us. The least broken and the most put together on any given day. Finn won't entertain the idea that he'll ever do anything disloyal.

"Do we need to talk about this?" He waves a hand between us.

"We share her. If it becomes a problem, we talk about it then."

Finn gives me a silent look of disbelief.

"Is it a problem now?" There's a testiness to my tone because I feel like I've been more than fair.

"Just that you've never been much for sharing."

"Not like we haven't before. That one vacation we took where everyone was paired up except the one chick when we got snowed in. What was her name? Brandy? Britney?"

"That was under unusual circumstances."

"And this isn't? We need her. She needs us. And we all have to believe that we won't fuck each other over." I pour myself a glass of whiskey and offer him one. He takes it, sipping it slowly where I take a long swallow and pour another.

"You know you can trust Hudson and me."

"And I can trust her more when I know where she sleeps and who she fucks."

"Oh yeah. That definitely seemed like a real fucking chore for you. Her suddenly icing out the professor will also help our cause."

"It certainly wasn't a fucking chore for you, was it?"

"I like her. Did before all this. I told you that upfront. I've never hidden that from you."

"So you want her to keep fucking the professor? Putting his grimy fucking hands all over her?" I try to derail this conversation. I don't have time for it.

"I'm just saying if you have feelings for her, be honest."

"I've always been honest with you. If I'm stupid enough to catch feelings over her, I'll let you know. Right now I just like how tight her cunt is and the way her tits bounce when she rides me. You're the one who wants to buy her fucking flowers."

"I might." A grin spreads over his face at the idea, and I shake my head. Another whisper of apprehension that I've driven the two of them together.

"Knock yourself out."

"I'm gonna go say my goodnights to people and then check on her and make sure she's okay after that."

I nod and watch him as he disappears out the door. He can buy her all the fucking flowers he wants to. I have other things I'll get her if I'm so inclined. Things only I can give her—like black-berries for one.

Seventeen

F^inn

I'm waiting for her, leaning against the door frame when she gets out of the shower, and she wraps the towel tighter around herself when she sees me. Her eyes shift to me nervously and this is exactly why I came in here.

"Hey," I say softly.

"Hey," she answers. "I was going to go to your room after I changed." She nods to the clothes she keeps in Rowan's closet. Another power move on his part when she moved in.

"I wasn't sure, and I just wanted to check on you."

She turns her back to me as she pulls underwear, a tee, and shorts out of a drawer in the closet and then shifts the towel to start putting them on. I walk up behind her, grabbing the sides of her shoulders and placing a kiss on the right one.

"Is it fucked up now?" she asks.

"Is what fucked up?"

"I don't know. A chance of something between us. I thought

there was one, at one point. Before Rowan..." she trails off, her fingers smoothing over the tattered edge of the old shirt she's holding.

"Rowan doesn't change anything."

She turns and looks at me, doubt coloring her face.

"I fucked your best friend in front of you."

"And it was hot as fuck."

"It doesn't bother you?"

"No. You and Rowan have your thing. We have ours." I run my fingers over her chin. "And I see the way you look at me."

"Stuff with Rowan, it's not the same. It's... I don't know. A power struggle I guess that apparently ends with us fucking it out if we don't fight." Her palm presses against my chest. "With you. It's something else entirely... It scares me honestly."

"Scares me sometimes too," I whisper, kissing her as she leans into me.

"Let's go to your room?" She looks around like Rowan might return at any minute, and I take her hand to reassure her, leading her back to my room.

When we step in, she looks around, smirking at the purple sheets and the purple walls.

"Favorite color or just a phase?" She grins.

"Favorite color."

"Mine too," she agrees absently as she picks up the mask I had on earlier in the evening, the same one we wore the night of the attempted robbery. Her fingers run over the ridges of the mask, her smirk refusing to fade.

"Something amusing you?"

"You looked hot in this mask. When I saw it was you... It uh... did things for me."

"The mask?"

"Yes." Color rises to her cheeks and her lashes darken her eyes as she puts it back on the dresser.

"Would it do things for you again if I wore it one night?" I ask curiously.

"I think I would like that."

"It can be arranged." It's my turn to smirk at her.

"Can it?" She reaches for my shirt, grabbing a handful of it, and pulls close to me.

"Yeah. I just need to think of what my equivalent is."

"Oh, a trade then?" She looks up at me.

"Yeah, something like that," I mumble because I'm too distracted by the way she's looking at me right now to think straight. The smell of her shampoo and the feel of her so close to me. Alone with me in this room where I've thought about her a half dozen times this week alone.

I reach down and grab her, pulling her feet up off the floor and depositing her on my bed. She lays back. Her violet hair fans out across the bed, blending in with the sheets where it falls on the parts that lay unmade. I climb up onto the bed with her, my hand running up under the tee she has on. Her skin is so soft, and I feel the way her muscles contract in the wake of my touch.

"I hated seeing you with those girls."

"I hated staying away from you."

"Why did you?"

"Rowan and I have an unwritten rule. If we both like the same girl, we stay away. Keeps the peace. And this time he was very clear about how he felt about me staying away from you."

"I hate him a little bit."

"I think the feeling's mutual." I smile and place a kiss on her stomach, her eyes shuttering with the sensation. I repeat it, and she takes a deep breath, letting it out slowly while I climb my way up her body, leaving a trail of goosebumps in my wake.

"Glad he broke the rules then," she mumbles.

"Me too," I whisper against her skin when I get to her neck, kissing her there and then moving to her jaw.

"Only sad I didn't get all of you."

"Do you want all of me?"

"Since the first day of class this year."

"Just this year? Damn. For me, it's been since that first class freshman year."

"Why didn't you ever say anything?"

"I didn't think I was your type. You didn't make any moves, and I'm used to girls coming to me."

"Ooooh, I get it." She laughs. "I mean I definitely saw that tonight. You don't have to work for much."

"I'd work for you." I take her lips with mine, kissing her softly at first, and then rougher as she wraps her arms around me and pulls me down. I nip her bottom lip, running my teeth over the plump lower one and then kissing my way down her again.

I'm going hard already with how good she feels underneath me, and she spreads her legs wider to let me settle between them, canting her hips up so she's cradling my cock, and I rock against her. Her eyes close, and she lets out a soft sound of approval.

"Do you want me to work for you?" I slide my hand between us, adjusting my cock until it's flush with her clit and moving my hips just enough that she can feel it.

"Yes. I want anything you give me, Finn." Something about the way she says my name sends a buzz through me, and now all I can think about is my mouth on her sweet little pussy. I grab her shorts and start to tug them down, pausing briefly to wait for permission, and she lifts her hips to help me get them off.

I kiss my way down her body, over her chest and stomach until I'm resting between her thighs, kissing her at first and then dragging my tongue through her wetness. So fucking gratifying that she gets this wet for me. That just that little bit of foreplay has her so ready for me. I use my tongue to massage her, dipping inside for a better taste before I slide my finger inside her while I suck her clit.

"Fuck... You taste like my new favorite thing, Duchess."

"Oh my god..." She moans when I suck on her again, and then use my tongue to give her more. "Don't you start too."

I smile to myself and then resume my torture, kissing, licking, sucking her, and using my fingers to keep her close to the edge.

"I need you inside me. I want to know what you feel like. Please, Finn."

That's all she has to do—ask and I'll jump. This girl already has that kind of control over me. I'm stripping down a moment later and then lining myself up with her. I tease her with the tip of my cock, sliding it over her clit and through her wetness to get myself ready for her. I'm bigger than average and the last thing I want is to hurt her. On the last round, I slide inside slowly, just the start of things to tease her.

She cries out, muttering how big I am and how full she feels. I begin to move then, letting her have a couple of inches at first, and then a few more. I fuck her slowly and carefully, gently pressing her thighs apart as I tell her how fucking beautiful she is.

"You're doing so well. Taking my cock like such a good girl, Charlotte. Feels *so fucking good*."

"More," she asks, and I follow her lead, giving her more on the next stroke and all of me on the one after that. When I'm all the way in she closes her eyes, taking a deep breath as I lean to kiss her throat. "Oh fuck. My neck... like that. Makes me so fucking wet when I feel your mouth on my throat like that."

I love her for being so vocal like this, telling me what she likes and what she wants. She was so quiet earlier with him. Having this different side of her now makes me feel like a fucking god. Like I get a special version of her that's only mine.

"Yeah? We need you soaking. You're so fucking tight, I barely fit."

She smiles. "But it feels so good. Like I'm going to be that good kind of sore tomorrow."

"Good." I suck a little hickey on her chest, and she squirms under the sensation.

"What was that for?" She raises a brow.

"I want to look at it when you're sauntering around the house in those little pajama shorts you wear and remember what it feels like when I'm this deep inside." I grin at her.

Her lashes flutter with amusement. I slide out of her and back in slowly again, giving her just enough to torment her.

"Fuck... Seriously just, fucking fuck..." She smiles and then her eyes close again, a soft moan coming before she catches my eyes again. "Fuck. Me. Hard."

I laugh but take her mouth with mine, kissing her as I start to move my hips, sliding out and back in again. I pick up the pace with a steady rhythm, loving how wet she is and how we sound when our bodies collide. Her breathing picks up the harder I take her.

"I'm almost—" Her warning is cut off when she starts to gasp as I grab one of her legs and change my position. "Oh my god. Finn. My god..." She turns into a mess of curses underneath me and the way her body shivers and clenches around my cock, I can't hold out anymore. She takes me with her, and I see fucking black from how hard I come, leaning forward, and bowing my head as I try to catch my breath. Kissing the side of her temple, cheek, and throat as I start to come down from it.

We stay like that for several minutes, letting our breathing even out before I slip out of her and collapse beside her on the bed.

"That was so good. *You* are so good." She looks over at me, and I grin.

"Yeah. You too."

Her lips quirk up at the side as she looks me over before she moves closer and kisses my cheek.

"You're kind of a softie, aren't you?"

"Under the right circumstances."

Her green eyes are so bright and her violet hair a tangled mess from the way we fucked. She looks so perfect like this—no makeup on, her tee pulled up at an awkward angle from the way I was touching her before. She might be the most gorgeous woman I've ever fucking seen and that thought makes me realize how fucked up I already am over her.

"I like these circumstances." She grins and then starts to sit up. "I'm gonna go get cleaned up. Really though... Do you mind if I sleep here? I don't have to. I can check and see if the couch is available or sleep in his bed."

"I'm pretty much going to demand it. That and cuddles." I kiss her elbow and she smiles at me again.

"All right. Cuddles it is."

EIGHTEEN

Charlotte

I sneak out to the kitchen to get a glass of water and a snack a couple of hours later when I wake up and can't go back to sleep. I'm honestly craving some more of the fruit Rowan had earlier and wondering if there's any still in the fridge. I doubt it though when I see the mayhem from the party left behind. Luckily Rowan's at least managed to kick everyone out, and I don't have to step over bodies or walk out to people fucking on my couch.

I do a double-take when I look over at it though because Rowan's there. His feet crossed and up on the coffee table, a bottle of Jack in his hand.

"You and Finn get your snuggles in and talk about how much you love each other?" He smirks, taking a long swig from the bottle.

"We fucked and fell asleep in his bed." I eye him warily.

"Fucked? You sure you didn't make love to him?" Rowan laughs to himself.

I ignore the bait and grab two bottles of water out of the fridge. I definitely don't expect the same sort of care that Finn takes with me from someone like Rowan, but him digging into me like this only a few hours after *we* fucked is a bit like salt in the wound.

"Why are you out here drinking alone and not in bed?" I ask, wrapping my fingers around the bottle of Jack, which he thankfully relinquishes without a fight, and replacing it with the water I've just uncapped for him.

"Alone's alone. Doesn't matter where it is." He takes a sip of the water.

My heart falters a little at the way he says it. I'm starting to wonder if maybe Rowan needed aftercare tonight.

"You need water and sleep. Not more Jack." I cap the bottle and put it back on the shelf before I sit down next to him.

"I need peace," he mutters, taking another swig of the water.

My lips twitch with amusement. "Are we at the drunk-enough-to-be-philosophical stage then? Maybe we should get you to bed." I reach for his hand, but he pulls it back.

"Still need more cock tonight?" A sneer pulls at the side of his mouth. "You're going to be exhausting."

I stare at him for a long minute, and he stares back. His face is a mask. One he wears well and not nearly as attractive as the one he had on before. I decide to hold my tongue, try to probe where this sudden wave of nastiness is coming from. Maybe I hurt him somehow. Did something I didn't realize that injured his heart or more likely his ego.

"Do we need to talk about this? Are you regretting it or what?" I turn toward him, studying his face.

"Regretting what? Using you like a fuckdoll with my best friend? Nah. We've done that plenty of times with other women. Although I will say you've got a tight little cunt. I see why the professor can't get enough."

"You're a fucking asshole." I stare at him. "I thought maybe..." I trail off. I don't know what I thought.

"Thought maybe your cunt would magically cure me? Christ, you're fucking naïve." He shakes his head, laughing to himself.

"I didn't think it would cure you of being an asshole. But I thought maybe us fucking meant this could be different." I point between us.

"Different how? That I'd suddenly be the same kind of lost puppy dog Finn is for you?" His face straightens, the laughs dissipating in favor of irritation.

I grab my water off the coffee table and go to stand, regretting ever coming out here to talk to him. His hand darts out far faster than anyone this drunk should be able to manage, grabbing the side of my neck and pulling me back down on the couch. I glare at him, but he just stares back, something in his eyes I can't read. His lips crash onto mine a second later.

His kiss is wild and rough, like he wants to prove a point and convince me all at the same time. He tastes like Jack but with a slightly sweet taste at the edge like the berries he'd eaten earlier. I'm melting back onto the couch while he climbs on top of me. His hand slips around the back of my head, his fingers threading through my hair, and his teeth graze along my throat before he kisses me again. His knee nudges my legs apart, and he settles between them. The seam of his jeans settling against me and pressing through the fabric of my panties where he's hard.

"You don't want different from me. You want me exactly the way I am. You just hate it. Hate me for things I can't change."

And he is definitely drunk if he's saying that.

"Only as much as you hate the fact you need me."

"That's a hell of a fucking lot."

"It's mutual."

He kisses me for a few more moments, alternating between rough and a softer sort of kiss that has me wishing he had a gentle side. After he's had his fill, he pulls away, his eyes drifting over my face like he's trying to find an answer.

"You better not fucking hurt him. I'll ruin you if you do."

He's talking about Finn, but I know he's talking about himself too. Even if he'll never admit it.

"No one's getting hurt. At least not other than Colin. We're getting the paintings. Getting our money and then getting out of this."

"And if he doesn't want you to go when it's done?"

"Then he'll have to convince me it's worth staying and putting up with you."

He collapses next to me on the couch on his side and then drags me close to him until our bodies are flush. He grabs the pillows that someone set on the back during the party and motions for me to lift my head, setting one down for each of us.

He uses the control on the side table to flick the overhead fan's light off and we're drenched in darkness. His arm wraps around my waist and he pulls me tight to him.

"What are we doing?"

"Sleeping."

"You didn't drink enough water."

There's a sigh that's half a rumbled growl.

He reaches over me, grabbing the water bottle I dropped when he kissed me, and chugs it down, tossing the bottle on the floor.

"Happy?"

"Better."

"Good. Now sleep." His arm returns to my waist, and I fall asleep to a quietly snoring Rowan at my back.

NINETEEN

harlotte

I've just gotten home from the diner when my phone dings with a text.

COLIN:

> I'm in town for the night until I leave again tomorrow. Brought something back for you. Come over?

I stare down at it, nibbling my lip as I climb the stairs and wondering how to answer him. I've been slowly ghosting him since the end of the semester and he hasn't made it very difficult. We've never been anything official. Just casual hookups and sleep-overs when it was convenient for his schedule. Whenever he was busy, I was discarded to the wayside, only to be picked up again when he was bored and desperate. Buying me presents—usually alcohol or chocolate—is his way of trying to buy himself back into my good graces. Not that I made it particularly difficult.

After all, he has something I want—it just isn't what he thinks it is.

I can't dump him yet. I don't need to draw his ire while we're still working on stealing his paintings. I'm hoping we can take them while he's gone in the coming weeks, but there's a chance we might need to do it while he's still home. And ideally, that would require me to be an invited guest.

I've been so deep in my thoughts, lost in my phone as I made my way through the house that I jerk back when I open the bathroom door to find steam rolling out. The shower's off but when I look to the side Rowan's standing there, a towel around his hips in front of the mirror at the sink shaving, a straight razor sliding along his jaw.

I'm stuck staring for a moment at his muscles and tattoos, the way his shoulders move, and how his bicep and forearm flex with each movement. I get a glimpse of his back tattoo—a massive raven with its wings spread across his shoulders.

"See something you like, Duchess?" He smirks without bothering to look at me.

"Sorry. I was distracted. Colin texted."

"And?" He takes another swipe down the sharp line of his jaw, and I follow the motion. I never realized a man shaving could be sexy, but apparently, Rowan's made it possible. At least with that jawline and those hands.

"He wants me to go over there tonight."

"No." His tone is flat, and his eyes flash to mine.

"I mean... I don't want to. But if I keep blowing him off, he's going to get annoyed or move on."

"Good. Let him find someone else to stick his dick in." He takes the final swipe along his cheek, setting the razor on the sink, and grabbing a wet washcloth to wipe the remnants of the shaving cream off his face.

"That won't help us. We need him until we get this done."

His jaw ticks, and he rinses the washcloth and hangs it over the bar before he turns to me.

"I was pretty clear the other night, wasn't I?" He closes the distance between us and my heart skips in my chest.

"Yes, but—"

"Yes, but," he repeats, mocking me. "But *nothing*. Tell him you're sick or had to go out of town."

"He'll lose interest if I keep putting him off, and then we'll have another problem on our hands."

"He won't lose interest if you call him and tell him how much you can't wait to have him inside you again. You don't have to go over there to feed him crumbs. You're clever. You've done it this long. You can do it a while longer."

I flash Rowan a look of irritation before I stare back down at my phone.

"I have to tell him something."

"Call him." It's the same tone he's used on Finn and Hudson before, a command—not a request.

I look up at him, and he holds my gaze, his eyes widening just enough to push me back into my place. I take a breath and unlock my phone. I don't usually call him, but Rowan's right. With us not having seen each other, this being more of a conversation will probably help ease any questions he's having about my avoiding him.

"Charlotte?" Colin answers the phone after only a couple of rings.

"Hi, Colin. How are you?"

"I'm fine. I was hoping to see you tonight."

"I know. That's why I'm calling. I'm actually out of town."

Rowan's brow jerks up like I'm doing a terrible job already.

"Oh. That's too bad. I was excited to give you the present that I brought back."

"I was excited to see you too. I just didn't know when you'd be back, and I had a... call from a... a friend. They invited me over for a few days. I'll be back soon, and we can get together then if you're interested." I stumble over my own words, far too unprepared for this conversation. The pressure from Rowan not helping.

"Of course I'm interested, Charlotte. But I have a meeting with some colleagues, and I'm headed back out of town for that. Then to see family for Christmas. I think we're going to miss each other. It's too bad."

"It is too bad," I answer. Rowan gives me a look like I need to lay it on thicker. "I was really hoping to see you. I can't stop thinking about you." The smirk returns to Rowan's face, and I glare at him.

"That's good to hear. I know I'm busy a lot, but I do think about you."

Rowan's grin grows, and I realize he can hear both sides of the conversation.

"Do you? How often do you think about me?" I roll my lower lip between my teeth and smile. Rowan's eyes snap to mine.

I hear Colin's breath catch on the other end of the line. I've caught him off guard. This isn't his strong suit. He's much more perfunctory about things. Discussions on the history of impressionism and the influence of patrons on artwork during the Renaissance are his version of dirty talk.

"Almost every night." I can hear the slight strain in his voice, like I'm pushing his comfort levels but he's curious where I'm headed.

"Tonight?"

"If you think I should."

"I do."

There's a pause on the line and then he clears his throat.

"You think you could send something to help with that? A photo maybe?"

I see the clench of Rowan's jaw and the way his cheek twitches in response to that idea. Which only makes me want to taunt him.

"I think so. I've never tried that. But I could try for you."

Rowan's nose raises with a sneer and his brow tightens as his eyes flick over me.

"I'd like that. A lot."

"All right. Well, I'll send something over in a few when I can get away," I say softly.

"Good. Think of me. I can't wait to see you when we're both back in town."

"Me too."

"Goodnight, Charlotte."

"Goodnight."

I press the button to disconnect and risk looking up at Rowan. He's not happy, but fuck is he sexy like this. Like he can't decide if he wants to kill me or fuck me.

"Problem?" I ask.

"Shouldn't make promises you can't keep."

"Like what?"

"You're not sending him photos of you."

"You heard him. Heard how his whole tone changed when I told him I would. You want him to stay interested, don't you? Feed him crumbs, right?"

"I want him to keep his hands and eyes off my things."

"I don't have a choice here, Rowan. I have to give him something."

"You're right. You do." The side of his mouth draws up in a smirk and his eyes rake over me. "Take those diner clothes off." I open my mouth to protest but his thumb slides over my lips. "For once in your fucking life, just do what I'm asking without opening that smart little mouth of yours. You'll like the reward."

I flash him a defiant look, but I set my phone down and start discarding my clothes until I'm down to my underwear. I glance at myself in the mirror. I look rough. My makeup looks like I've worn it all shift. My hair's starting to tumble out of the bun I put it up in this morning. The underwear I have on is more functional than sexy, a soft gray cotton set that's comfortable on days like today when I'm running around like crazy covered in grease, pop, and milkshake spatter. Definitely nothing the professor's going to find attractive. That was another thing he always got me along with the wine and chocolate. Everything tight and lacy and barely there. He balked the first few times I stayed over and wanted to sleep in regular PJs and only allowed it if I dressed up for him first.

"I need to change if I'm going to take photos. He's picky about lingerie and he'll hate this. Probably should do lipstick too." I move to head to the closet, but Rowan catches my wrist and pulls me back toward him, pinning me between him and the counter. His eyes rake over me in the mirror.

"Fuck him," he whispers against my ear. "I like you like this. I want you exactly like this." His lips are at my throat.

"Rowan..." It's half-protest and half-request for more.

His hand slips under my bra and his palm grazes over my nipple.

"You're right, Duchess. We gotta give him something. I know the perfect fucking thing." His free hand slips down to my phone where it's still unlocked, and he opens the sound recording app there. I give him a questioning look in return. He answers by slipping his hand under the elastic of my panties, the pads of his fingers gently sliding over my clit. "Just like the night in the closet. Only when you're all wet, soaking these panties and gasping over how good it feels, you're going to hit record."

"Rowan... that's not going to work."

"Not if you say my name like that. I know how much you like it but this once, Duchess, you can't. It's a challenge but I think you can handle it."

"Can *you* handle being quiet while we're recording?" I goad him in return.

"Knowing how deep I'm going to bury myself in this cunt after? Yeah. I'm good."

His pace picks up, and he alternates between teasing the edges of my clit between his spread fingers and giving me more direct friction. I lean back, my eyes closing for half a moment at how good it feels before I reopen them. His gray eyes burn into me, watching every breath and movement I make. Reading me like he's taking notes for future opportunities, but he stays quiet like he promised.

He's still in his towel, and I reach for the edge of it, lifting my eyes to meet his. He smirks, and I tug the edge, letting it drop to the floor. He nods to my bra, and I reach back to unhook it, letting it slip off into the pile we're creating at our feet. His lips pull up on one side in appreciation, and I can't help the answering smirk on my part. One he seems to both hate and like as his fingers dip inside and his thumb strokes over my clit.

I bite my tongue, but a moan slips out anyway. He's already gotten me to the edge, little sparks of pleasure blooming and ebbing as he alternates his motions, and I can feel how wet I'm getting by how easily his fingers glide over me.

"Turn around and put the phone on the counter right in front of you. I want him to hear everything. The way you moan. How wet I make you."

I follow his instructions, my finger hovering over the record button.

"Now," he demands, and I press it.

A moment later he intensifies the pressure and rhythm he has on my clit, and I'm bracing my hands on the counter, breathing heavily as I listen to the sound of his fingers slipping over me. I drag my panties down further over my hips, so he has better access. While he keeps his promise and doesn't say a word, the deep breath he takes is a reward of its own.

He pulls me closer, pressing his cock against my ass as he takes on a punishing pace with his fingers. I watch the flex of his forearm, and I can't help the next moan that comes out, followed by a gasp as my orgasm starts to hit hard. I reach back, grabbing his cock and stroking it to the same rhythm he's using on my clit. Desperate to break him like he's breaking me right now. But he doesn't stop and doesn't make a single sound—not while my vision goes blurry and I shut my eyes, not while I gasp and whimper, and not while I moan loudly through the last wave of it. But when I open my eyes again his fingers slip out of me, and he presses the stop button on the recording.

I'm still catching my breath when he sends it to Colin and then reopens it again, hitting play. It's quiet at first and then he turns up the volume until the sounds of it echo against the tile in the room.

"Bend over and spread your legs, Duchess. I wanna hear you come again to the sound of me getting you off. I want it in fucking stereo."

My cheeks heat when I hear the sounds of him finger fucking me on my own phone, but I bend like he asks, and he slides inside me. And like I haven't had enough already, he wraps his hand around my hair and pulls, bringing his lips to my ear.

"And this time you're gonna listen to every fucking sound I make."

He fucks me hard and rough, and I have to brace myself more than once before he pulls me back up again and takes me harder on the next round.

"Listen to you. How desperate you are when I touch you. How hard you fucking come. So fucking greedy for anything I give you."

"Fuck..." I gasp because I can feel the edge of another orgasm, and I'm desperate to chase it. I slip my fingers over my clit, and he smirks at the state he's put me in.

A moment later he comes hard, gripping my hips and then pulling me closer to him. He slips out of me and grabs my jaw, nipping his way down the edge of it. I turn the recording off. His eyes track down to my thighs in the mirror, another grin on his face as he kisses me.

"Fuck I love watching my come drip out of you." He dots another kiss on my jaw. "Keep that recording too. We'll use it again sometime."

"Rowan..."

"Duchess..." He smacks my ass and then turns on the shower for me. "You sleep in my bed tonight."

He cleans himself up and then heads out, leaving me to take my shower. My phone dings a moment later, and I open the text assuming it's him with another taunt from the bedroom. But it's not.

COLIN:

I love it. I'll send you one later.

TWENTY

When I get in that evening after going to my video game night, I tuck my phone in my pocket before I toss my bag on the floor next to the rest of the gear the guys have lying inside the door. I make my way through the kitchen and into the living room. It's oddly dark in the house. Normally at this hour Rowan and Finn are playing a video game or watching a movie, propped up with snacks and drinks on the couch. Since Charlotte's made her home here, she's usually with them or at the kitchen table working on something.

I notice the strip of dull light coming through the pocket doors that lead to the office Rowan's claimed for himself, and I see a flash of movement through the sliver of the opening. They must be in there working on the plan or prepping for something, and I'm a little pissed I've been left out of the equation. So I don't think twice when I pull the pocket door, half-ready to give them shit. Not remotely expecting what I see there, my heart jolts in my chest and all the blood in my body floods south.

Charlotte's on the leather couch, completely fucking naked and on all fours, her face between Rowan's thighs. Rowan's sitting on the arm of the couch, his hand wrapped around a fistful of her hair as she takes him in her mouth. Her lips are over him in rhythm with the thrust of Finn's hips as he kneels on the other side of the couch, fucking her from behind. She moans as he fucks her harder and all of it—the sight of it, the sounds of her, the realization the three of them are fucking and I'm an outsider to this (and worst of all a massive surge of jealousy) hits me at once like a fucking freight train of adrenaline.

I hear ringing in my ears, and I go to turn quickly. I want to get out of here before they see me. Because the second they look at me—the second *she* looks at me—the jealousy is going to be written all over my face. I feel bitter enough without being embarrassed on top of it.

Unfortunately, I'm too fucking graceless and forget where the door is, slamming my nose into it. I fucking yelp loudly just before the black at the edges fades in, and I hit my knees feeling like I'm about to pass out from the pain. Somewhere in the periphery, I hear the three of them gasp and call out for me, followed by a blur of movement. I lift my head and blood's pouring out my nose like I've just been hit on the ice.

I think I fucking want to die here.

"Jesus Fucking Christ." Rowan's come over and is staring at me like I'm an idiot until the sight of the blood makes his brow crease into worry. "Did you fucking break it?"

"Oh my god. Hudson!" Charlotte's tone is all concern, and she's on her knees next to me a moment later, covered up in Finn's oversized shirt. "Are you okay? Oh my god. Okay well someone go get some towels. And hurry! He's bleeding everywhere. Ice too. Shit, Hudson. What happened?"

Her hands cup under mine, catching some of the blood that's

dripping down over my fingers and trying to keep it from landing on my clothes. It's humiliating, and I start to pull away.

"Don't move." Her hand goes to my shoulder to stop me while the other one continues to try to stop the blood. "Let Finn get a towel first."

"It's fine. I'm fine."

"You're not fine."

She's right. I'm not fine because I'm fucking hard, still, and bleeding out my face after having interrupted their fucking threesome.

"Here." Finn's hand is suddenly in front of me holding a towel, and I blot at my nose. "Use pressure or it won't stop."

He would know. He's had enough nose bleeds and broken noses to be a PhD level expert on them.

"I'll get some ice." Charlotte stands, and all I see is skin—all the way up her long legs to her thighs—and a flash of more under that shirt. I close my eyes.

"I know it fucking hurts." Finn tries to reassure me. "It'll get better once she gets some ice for you."

There's not enough fucking ice in the world right now. I needed fucking buckets of it. Maybe a whole tub I could submerge myself in. I've already felt guilty as fuck for crushing on Charlotte. Soph has been so distant lately. Barely wanting to talk to me or answer my texts. Never wanting to video chat. It's been two weeks since I've even heard her voice.

Being alone all the fucking time with my thoughts is hard as fuck. I've been trying desperately to think of Soph whenever I get myself off, but Charlotte is always there at the edges of my mind creeping in. I've imagined what she'd look like naked and none of my fantasies have lived up to the real thing. This is going to be difficult as fuck to block out from my memory, and I need to.

A moment later she's on her knees again, a pack of ice out of the freezer on hand. We have enough injuries in this house after games that we keep it stocked.

"Here, why don't we get you up? You can sit on the couch," she offers.

"Yeah, no thanks." I flip a look to Finn and Rowan.

Finn just grins but the arrogant smirk on Rowan's face wears on my nerves.

"Here." Rowan grabs his office chair and pushes it in my direction.

I start to stand, and Charlotte's hands wrap around my bicep, doing her level best to support me. More humiliation washes over me that she has to help at all.

"I'm good," I reassure her quietly.

"You're not good. I can help. Here... you hold the towel, and I'll hold the ice." She's leaning over me, one leg on either side of my knee. The smell of her shampoo and sex envelops me.

"I've got it," I insist, trying to take the ice pack and adjust my cock, so she doesn't see or feel how hard I am.

"Just let me help," she huffs, a tinge of irritation to the reassuring tone in her voice.

"That's not the kind of help he wants, Duchess," Rowan muses, his eyes dancing with a taunt as he studies me.

"What?" Charlotte's too focused on the ice pack and my face to understand his meaning.

He comes up behind her and slides his hand under the shirt she's wearing, the motion raises it up enough to give me a flash of what's underneath, and I avert my eyes.

She's my friend. We're *friends*. I have a girlfriend. A girlfriend who doesn't seem to fucking want me to be her boyfriend. But still a fucking girlfriend in name anyway.

"Rowan..." She gasps and her eyes close as his hand slips between her legs. "I'm trying to..." Her voice fades as she swallows, and I look past her to Rowan—his eyes hard set as he watches me watching them.

"You can help him take his mind off the pain. Let him finish watching you get fucked the way you need it." Rowan's eyebrow raises in question, wanting to silently confirm what he suspects.

Fucking help me because I don't say no. Her eyes flutter open, and she looks at me, confusion marring her face. I can barely stand to look at her when her eyes meet mine, the question there in them. She rolls her lower lip between her teeth and her brows knit together, but Rowan pulls her backward.

"Come on, Duchess. Let's finish you off. Let him see how well you take me and Finn."

Fuck. I want to leave. I want to stay. I want to run, and I want to watch. But instead I'm just stuck here, glued to the chair while Rowan hands her off to Finn again.

Finn takes his shirt back, exposing her again, but her eyes never leave mine. I pull the towel away, the blood slowing now that I have the ice pack and it falls to my lap. I absently run my palm over myself through my sweats and her eyes fall hard on the motion. There's not much left to the imagination, because I'm rock fucking hard now, and Rowan's right. I've forgotten the throbbing sensation in my face because I can only think about the one that's between my fucking legs. Dying to be put out by watching her.

Finn's taken on Rowan's role, his hand between her legs as she leans back against him. I can tell how wet she is by the way she coats his fingers each time he strokes them over her clit, and she writhes under his touch. A few muted moans reach me all the way over here like they're climbing up my spine and invading every sense I have.

Rowan's pulling himself back out, stroking his cock and watching Finn torment her. This must be the reason the tension between them has dropped from its former sky-fucking-high state. Finn and Rowan have somehow come to a fucked-up compromise over her. It's all making sense now.

Her eyes are still fixed on me though, and I shift mine to the floor again. I've never felt so fucking conflicted in my life. So turned on by something that feels wrong.

"You can watch." Rowan's tone is muted, and when I look up his fingers are running through her hair as she looks up at him.

"You don't care if he watches, do you?" He looks down at Charlotte, she shakes her head no, and then looks at me.

"You can stay... if you want," she offers softly.

My heart skips in my chest, and my fingers flex around the ice pack. There's a question in her eyes like she's wondering if I like this or if I'm judging her for it. And fuck, I'm not at all. I'm just thinking how much I wish I could be a part of it. That she'd ever look at me the way she looks at them.

I should leave. Put distance between myself and this whole scene. Give myself time to process. But I want to watch her come, even if it's not me who's taking care of her. I want to see what she looks like. I want her to know I'm watching and loving every fucking second of it.

I don't move to leave, and I see the telltale smirk on Rowan's face. His hand cups her chin and his thumb slides over her lips.

"You need to finish what you started, Duchess. Let me coat this throat of yours. Show Hudson how well we can all get along when we want to."

Her tongue slides over him then before she takes him in her mouth, and a moment later, I watch as Finn's hand slides over her ass and down her thigh before he slides inside her again. He shudders, and his jaw tightens when he's all the way inside. I've never had a bad thought toward Finn in my life, but I might hate him now. Just a little bit—and a bit more when he starts to fuck her, and she moans softly around Rowan's cock. Her hand fists around him as she sucks him, and Rowan closes his eyes as he mutters little muted phrases of praise as she works on him.

But it's the thing that happens next that changes the fucking chemistry in my brain forever.

Her eyes open and they lock on mine for a moment before they drift down to where I'm absently pressing my palm over my cock. I'm so fucking hard, and so desperate I'm imagining it's her mouth on me. Her hand strokes down over him and her eyes lift to meet mine and drift down once more. Almost like she's encouraging me.

So I fucking do the thing I shouldn't. I slide my hand under the band of my sweats and grab my cock. I close my eyes, too self-conscious not to when I give it a slow stroke. At least until I hear her again. Another soft moan, and I dare myself to open them again, meeting hers and she's watching me intently. I stroke myself again and another moan follows from her.

Rowan's fingers tighten in her hair, and he mutters something, but I can't hear him. Not really. Because I'm too busy watching her as her free hand slides between her legs, and she starts to rub her clit—her eyes never leaving mine. And now I know I'm fucked. Because I don't care that Finn's fucking her or Rowan's cock is in her mouth. Her fingers are on her pussy for me because she's watching me stroke my cock under my sweats, and she fucking *likes* it. Likes me watching her. Likes that I can't control myself while I do it.

Fuck me.

It won't take much more. This whole scene is too much for me. I'm not practiced enough, and I'm still fucking lightheaded from the pain of smashing my face into the door. Every single stroke of my hand over my cock has everything in me going tight and hard, desperate to fucking come.

Watching her I can tell it's the same for her. Charlotte's eyes are locked on the place where my hand slides back and forth under my sweats, and her fingers follow my rhythm, her hips rolling back against Finn to the same beat and despite the fact I'm halfway across the room I feel like all of it is for me.

"Fuck..." she moans as she pulls away from Rowan for a moment. "I'm so close."

"You're doing so fucking well, Charlotte. So fucking gorgeous getting fucked by both of us," Finn offers her words of encouragement.

"That's right Duchess. You're our perfect little fuckdoll. Taking both our cocks at the same time. Now finish sucking me off. I want my cock in your mouth when you come for us. Want you to choke on it when you try to scream my name."

Rowan's rougher with her, but she looks up at him with lust in her eyes.

"Ask me nicely," she taunts him, and fuck if the way she says it doesn't do things for me.

He smirks at her but relents.

"Please suck my cock and let me come down your throat."

She smiles before she takes him again, deeper than ever before, and he groans loudly.

"God damn, Duchess. Your mouth... Fuck me."

"You close, Charlotte? I'm gonna fucking come." Finn's hand slides over her lower back and ass again, kneading the flesh there as she leans back into him. She moans her approval, her fingers back on her clit again. She glances at me like she wants to make sure I'm still in it, and I can't help the small smile that flits over my lips. One it almost seems like her eyes return before Finn starts to fuck her harder. Her full breasts bounce with every movement, and I imagine sliding underneath her to lick her sweet pussy. Letting her fuck my face for relief while they fuck her. The imaginary scene's too fucking good, and I can't take anymore, feeling the rush of my own orgasm distracting me as I use my hand to take me over the edge of it.

It's a blur after that. Finn and Rowan groaning as they start to fill her up, her moaning as her fingers slip over her clit again and again, and the feeling of my own release warm and wet on my hand as I see black at the edges of my vision from how hard I just came.

I watch her as she collapses, and Finn catches her, pulling her into his lap. Her head slips under his chin, and he kisses her forehead while he praises her for how perfect she is. Rowan stands to grab some tissues off the shelf and cleans himself up. I don't miss the way he watches them, a tinge of jealousy and want on his face when he sees the same thing I am—the easy way she clings to Finn like he's her lifeline. As if it might be more than just his cock she likes so much.

I realize I don't belong here anymore. How fucking awkward

this all is now that the haze of desperation is starting to fade, and I stand abruptly. Charlotte and Finn are so engrossed in each other they don't even notice but Rowan looks up at me. His eyes flash over me, and we exchange a look. The kind that recognizes we're both sick fucking bastards for wanting her.

Then I rush off for the shower. I'd needed one before, and after that—knowing full well how often it's going to play and replay in my mind for the rest of my life—I definitely need one now.

TWENTY-ONE

C harlotte

When we get to Colin's house it's surprisingly easy to get in, and all four of us slip in the same way they had the last time. The difference is that this time he is well and truly gone. I confirmed it on a phone call with him earlier in the evening when I wished him a Merry Christmas. The house is dark and completely silent, and we do our best to work with the ambient lighting in the room until we get to the paintings. The last thing we need to do is attract the attention of the neighbors.

Everyone disperses to their assignments just like we've practiced a million times before tonight. Hudson slips off to check that we've disarmed all the cameras in and around the house and make sure we haven't been caught on any of them on the way in. Rowan and Finn work to pull the paintings down from their frames while I work on getting the fakes set up to go in.

I had a wild idea at the last second—one Finn and I were able to realize in the art department's new lab. Late in the evening hours when the studio rooms are all still open for people to work on an honor system but are mostly a ghost town at that hour.

When Colin had shown us these paintings, and bragged about how he got them and their history, he shared photos in the slides. Ones he saved on a drive that he let students have access to in case they missed class or just wanted to revisit the lectures before a test. I clicked on one of the photos, praying that the man had been stupid enough to upload high-resolution photos. And he did—original scans he had done in incredibly high resolution that he'd then saved.

I remembered when he showed them in class that they took time to load, which had been odd. That memory paid off when the scans were large enough to create full-scale reproductions on the art lab's oversized printer. One we logged into with his code. So if the man was ever smart enough to figure out the real paintings had been taken, and he filed for insurance, he'd look like the fraud if they did any real sort of investigation. It's so poetic that I almost want to shed a tear at our handiwork.

We work fast having practiced with the copies in our living room at least four times the previous week to make sure we could get in and out fast. Hopefully, everyone is too busy with their Christmas celebrations to even notice anything outside their own homes, but just in case we need to be quick.

The copies go in easily, and Rowan and Finn get them back up on the wall just as Hudson returns from the other rooms.

"All clear," Hudson whispers before he glances up at the paintings. "Fuck, those are good."

"That's the plan." I smile at my handiwork.

"Good thing we have you." He grins back at me, and Rowan flashes a look at both of us before they mount the final painting on the wall.

"Not bad," Finn comments as he steps back.

"All right. We should get out of here." Rowan nods to the door.

Each of us takes one of the paintings and puts it in a tube we brought the fakes in, tucking them under our coats. We all hurry back out the door, into the dead of night on Christmas Eve. The cold air whipping in and around us as we walk down the street. Hudson starts to hum bars from Merry Christmas Baby as I grin in his direction.

"Hush. We can celebrate when we get back," Rowan grumbles at him.

"Well, we know who the Grinch is," Hudson jokes.

"Why do we live with them again?" Finn takes my hand.

"I think we like them. Maybe? Most of the time?" I smile up at him because I'm going to scream for joy the second we get back to the house. Blast some Christmas music and dance around the house to it. Somehow it seems like we might actually pull this off.

Twenty-Two

F inn

That morning when I get up, I'm the first one down. I see the stockings Charlotte's put by the fireplace with our names on them, and I grin. It had been a long night last night, and I assume the rest are all in bed until I hear Rowan's voice.

"What are you grinning about?" He sounds groggy and half-awake as he stumbles down the steps.

"She made us all stockings." I reach for mine and pull it off the hook before I look up at him. "She awake yet?" She went to sleep in his bed last night I assume because she isn't down here on the couch.

"No. She's still passed out. Took a shower last night and collapsed on the bed. I was going to get coffee started before I wake her."

"She okay after last night though?"

"Far as I know. Like I said, didn't talk to her much yet."

I raise my eyebrow when I pull open the stocking because

tucked inside is a black balaclava, some candy canes, black gloves, and a bottle of flavored lube.

"What?" Rowan asks from the kitchen when he sees my brows raise.

"Look in yours and tell me what's inside." I nod my head toward his stocking. He frowns but turns the coffee maker on before he saunters over.

"Why? What did you get?" He peers over my shoulder as he grabs his stocking. I hold up the contents and there's a flash of amusement before he hurries to open his. He pulls out a matching set of mask and gloves, more candy canes, and a set of velvet, candy-striped ribbons.

"Holy fuck. She's something else."

"You think they were meant to be our gift or hers?" I muse.

"I think I know how we're waking her up." He smirks.

"Get her some coffee first," I warn as I pull the tags off the masks and gloves.

A few minutes later we're hurrying up the stairs clad in masks and gloves while we suck on the candy canes she gave us. He pushes the door back quietly, but the slight squeak of the hinge has her stirring. She turns over and blinks when she sees us, sitting up abruptly. It takes her a second but neither of us has a shirt on and once she recognizes our tattoos she relaxes.

"Found your stocking stuffers then?" Her voice is raspy from sleep, and it does things for me. A soft grin forms on her lips and my heart twists with it. This girl has me by the balls whether she knows it or not. She's all I can think about lately.

"Something like that." I set the lube and the velvet ribbon on one nightstand while Rowan sets the coffee on the one closest to her.

"And coffee? What a gentleman." Her eyes flick over Rowan, and her smile widens.

"I'm a lot of things, Duchess. Gentle ain't fuckin' one of

them." He kneels on the bed and wraps his hand around her throat. "But you don't want gentle. Not when you leave us things like this. You want us both to ravage this sweet fucking body, don't you?"

Her eyes flick over to me, drifting down over my chest and then back to him.

"Yes."

"Good."

"You want to tell us what you want, or you just want us to take it?" I ask because I want to be sure we're playing the game she wants.

Her eyes meet mine, full of lust and maybe even more importantly the trust she has in us—in me. "Take it. How you want."

I roll my lower lip between my teeth and tilt my head. "What she wants, she gets. Especially Christmas morning. You don't like something, or you want us to stop, you just say Santa, got it?"

"Santa. Got it." She grins, taking a sip of the coffee before Rowan takes it from her and puts it back on the nightstand.

I slide onto the bed, ditching the candy before grabbing her and pulling her into my lap. She's only in an oversized T-shirt and panties, and Rowan's hands go for them immediately. He drags them down her legs while I lift her shirt up over her head and toss it to the side. I pull the mask up just enough that my lips can creep up her spine and around the side of her throat. She gasps at the contact and then lets out a soft moan when I start to suck on the flesh at the base of her throat, leaning back against me as she spreads her legs.

I cup both of her breasts, running her nipples between my index fingers and thumbs while Rowan crawls between her thighs. He spreads them wider, and her lashes flutter open again, so she can watch him as he lays her out. He pulls his mask up like I have and runs his tongue through the wetness already coming after just a few touches.

"So fucking dirty for us, Duchess," I whisper against her ear. "You want us both this morning?"

"Yes," she whispers back, sucking in a breath a second later when he sucks on her clit. One of her hands threads through Rowan's hair, and the other slides behind her back and down between us where she palms me through my sweats.

"Setting up our stockings like that. All so you can get what you want for Christmas. Clever." I pinch one of her nipples, and she moans softly, her head lulling back against my shoulder as she rolls her hips toward Rowan's face. I'm jealous he gets to taste her first, but she's so sweet and so desperate right now that I don't know if I could restrain myself the way he is.

"I thought it was." A small smirk forms on her face.

"What'd you put in Hudson's?"

"You mean he's not coming too?" I can tell she's kidding and the way her eyes drift down to Rowan I know she's done it on purpose. He pulls away from her, raising an eyebrow as he sits back on his heels.

"You're going to pay for that one."

"Counting on it," she sasses back, and I grin against her skin before I kiss her. Glancing up to see Rowan's eyes darken.

He grabs her jaw and then pulls the candy cane out of the cup where he stashed it. He slides it over her tongue.

"Suck," he demands, and she does, swirling her tongue over it and taking it deeper each time like she's taunting him. Right before she bites the tip off, crunching it between her teeth as another grin forms. His grip on her jaw tightens, and he takes the candy cane away from her, biting off a piece himself. He chews for a moment while he studies her. Then his fingers slip down, and he pulls her forward by her neck.

"If you're gonna be a brat, we'll have to fuck some sense into you. Turn around." She does as he says, backing her ass up against him and winking at me as she does it. "Pull Finn's cock out."

She looks to me for permission, and I nod. Her hands are there a second later, greedily stroking over me and bending down to lick the precum off the tip. I groan and close my eyes, letting my head fall back against the headboard. She sucks me tentatively, like she's teasing me, and I hear Rowan grunt his disapproval.

I open my eyes just in time to see him wrap a fistful of her hair around his hand and press her forward. She takes my cock deep then, so deep I can feel the back of her throat, and he guides her mouth over me. Back and forth at a punishing pace until I feel her gag and see the tears start to form in her eyes.

"Charlotte?" I ask, her eyes meeting mine before she hums a little noise of approval. "Fuuuuck me." I groan at the way it vibrates along my cock.

"Spread your legs for me," he demands, and she follows his order. He lets go of her then, sliding back on the bed, admiring her body from a new angle.

She pulls back off my cock for a second and looks up at me, still stroking me. "I love how big you are. How you feel in my mouth."

Rowan takes his gloves off, tossing them to the side before his hand comes down hard on her ass. She grunts against the pain, her hand momentarily tightening around my cock.

"Fuck..." she mutters, closing her eyes tight before she opens them again and gives me a conspiratorial look. "That wasn't hard enough. Try again?"

The grin on Rowan's face looks positively evil, and he smacks her on the other side. He pulls his pants down then, stroking his cock before he lines up against her.

"You want this tight cunt full of my cock while you suck him off?"

"Yes. Please," she begs before her tongue slides over me again.

"I want something in return though," he says as he slides his fingers over her clit, and her hips buck at the contact.

"Anything," she murmurs before she sucks on the tip of my cock again.

"I want to show Finn what we've been working on." A devious grin spreads across Rowan's face when my eyes snap up to his. "Drawer." He nods to the nightstand, and I open it.

Inside is an anal vibrator, and I glance down at her, raising a brow.

"She wants to take us both at the same time. So we've been working her up to it," Rowan explains.

Her cheeks heat, and she stops for a minute to look up into my eyes, pulling away to speak. "If you want to. I just thought—"

"Yes. Fuck yes," I answer because I don't need an explanation. The idea of her taking us both has me so fucking turned on I can't handle thinking about it more. I just want to do whatever she wants—whatever she needs to make it happen for her.

"See, Duchess, I told you he'd like it. The thought of you being so fucking full of us both."

I hand her the vibrator and lube, and she hands it back to him. Her lashes flutter again when she turns back to me, a shy smile plays at her lips before she takes me in her mouth again.

"I can't imagine a woman more perfect than you. This body. This mouth. How sweet you are to us," I run the backs of my knuckles against her cheek, and she takes me deep, using her tongue and her mouth to work me over as Rowan slides inside her. I watch as he lubes her and the toy up, pressing it gently against her ass and turning it on. I can tell the moment she feels it because she sucks on me even harder, moaning as her hand tightens around me.

"Oh fuck..." I mutter, my fingers raking through her hair and tightening, pulling her back gently. "Careful or I'll come before I get my turn inside that sweet little pussy, and I need it."

She gives me a sheepish look and pulls back again, teasing the tip of my cock and stroking me just gently enough to keep me on the edge. I watch Rowan slide the toy inside her slowly, adding more lube and watching for her reaction. He's fucking her so slowly and gently it's almost hard to believe it's him. But he's just as fucked up over her as I am, even if he doesn't want to admit it. Desperate to please her and give her any little thing she wants so long as she keeps her big green eyes on us.

We stay like that for several minutes, him warming her up

slowly until she can take the whole toy and she's bucking back against him desperately begging for more of it and his cock.

"You ready?" I slide my fingers under her chin, and she pulls back and nods.

"I want to hear you say it, Duchess."

"I'm ready. I want both of you. Now."

I lose my pants and Rowan follows suit, tossing his mask to the floor. When I climb back on the bed she straddles me, lining herself up before she takes my cock. Her whole body shudders, and she gasps when she's full of me.

"Fuck your cock is so big, Finn." She raises her hips and slides over me once, twice, and braces her hands on my shoulders. "I don't know how you'll both fit."

Twenty-Three

C harlotte

Finn's dick always feels a little too big until I'm too lost in fucking him to remember. But right now with my nerves on edge over taking them both, and hopefully not being a complete mess while we do it has me clenching down so tight, I can't imagine anything else. I'm too full as it is. But Rowan's hands are on my back, running down my spine, little circles of reassurance before they go firm and press me forward.

"You can do it, Duchess. You can do it for us. Just think about how good it's going to feel when we're both inside, filling you up." Rowan's mouth trails its way down my neck and then he nips his way along my shoulder.

I roll my hips to slide over Finn's dick again, and it already feels so good I can't imagine more. At least until Rowan slides a lubed finger inside, and I gasp.

"Oh my god. Oh fuck." I murmur as he starts to move it,

adding another to the mix as Finn takes one of my nipples in his mouth.

"You like that? The way it feels when you let me have this?" Rowan whispers against my ear.

"Yes."

"Good. I need this, Duchess. Need to know I was the first you let have this. So perfect and tight for me. The first time we share like this."

"This is your first like this?" I ask, shocked because Rowan had always made it seem like they did this on the regular. I look to Finn because while I trust Rowan, I know Finn couldn't lie to me.

"Never like this." Finn shakes his head, his hand cradling my jaw before he kisses me. It's long and slow like he wants to remind me of the things he has that Rowan doesn't. The parts of me he owns in ways Rowan can't.

I roll my hips and take him deeper as Finn's tongue tangles with mine, and I feel Rowan's cock slide through the generous amount of lube he's used. I brace my hands on Finn's shoulders as Rowan starts to slide in, so slow and careful it's almost like he's channeling Finn.

"Oh fuck me, Duchess. You're so fucking tight. Like a fucking vice. Fucking fuck." Rowan groans.

I take deep breaths and start to slide down slowly on his cock, gradually letting myself adjust to the sensation of having them both. Finn's mouth slides over my jaw and throat, and Rowan's hand massages my hip.

"You're doing so good for us. Such a good fucking girl. Just like that," Finn whispers against my skin, the pads of his fingers gently teasing my clit.

I slip down further and choke on a gasp when I finally have them both inside me. It's so overwhelming. So much I feel like I might come on the spot from how much I feel all at the same time. My heart picks up a rhythm in my chest, and I feel like it might burst.

"Fucking hell." Rowan curses against my shoulder, his fingers biting into my hip as I start to test how it feels to move.

I slowly slide up and then down again, just the tiniest bit, and I can't help the moan that comes out of me. So fucking loud I'm sure the neighbors down the block probably heard it. Hudson had to.

"It's so much."

"You okay?" Finn asks.

"Yes, just… I'm going to come so fast when I start to move."

Finn grins and kisses me, nipping at my lower lip. "That's okay. You're going to take me with you."

I kiss him one more time and then I start to move in earnest taking them a little faster with each try until they're both moaning. Rowan's hand wraps around my hair and his other hand grabs my ass, supporting me as I come down. Finn's mouth is at my throat and over my breasts, licking, sucking, and biting his way until I don't know where any of us begin and end. Rowan was right when he said they were going to ruin me. I can't imagine not having them—both of them.

Finn's fingers work my clit, massaging me gently at first and then picking up his pace as I start to fuck them faster. Rowan starts to counter my strokes and it doesn't take much before I'm coming harder than I ever have in my life. Rowan's right behind me, his teeth sinking into my shoulder, and his hand around my throat as he groans his release. Finn's just another moment after us, cursing as he comes.

Rowan slides out of me slowly, and I ride out the last wave of my orgasm on Finn's cock. Just as he's slipping out of me, I hear the groan of a floorboard in the hall and look up to see a glimpse of Hudson. I wonder how much of us he caught. But I don't have much time to dwell on it before my attention is brought back to the two men I can't seem to get enough of.

I feel so sated and so empty at the same time right now, feeling the warmth of both of them slipping down my thighs. I collapse in a sweaty mess at Finn's side, turning over on my back next to him to look up at Rowan. He's still on his knees, breathing heavily as his eyes rake over my body.

"Holy fuck. I don't think I've ever seen anything hotter than you covered in both of us like this—our come, our sweat. Our dirty little Duchess." He smirks.

Finn leans over, kissing his way down my shoulder. "That was the hottest fucking sex of my life."

"Yeah..." I agree. "And the most exhausting." I grin before I close my eyes.

Rowan collapses next to me, throwing an arm over my waist. "No sleeping yet. Shower. Breakfast. Then you can sleep for a bit before we fuck you again."

"Again?" I raise a brow at him.

"Yeah. I already know what I want for being such a good fucking boy and giving you this." Another devious smile is on his lips, and I can hardly look at him without returning it.

"I think we might need to work on your definition of good boy. But what's that?"

"I'm gonna fuck you with this mask on while you watch me in the mirror. Take turns with Finn like you're our dirty little whore until we both fill you up. And then I want to watch you use our come to play with yourself."

"Rowan..."

"That's right, Duchess. Say my name. We both know it's mine you want to scream. Finn will just have to get used to it."

"Fuck off, Rowan," Finn grunts. "It's me she's been thinking about for the last year when she touches herself."

"All right, Duchess. Settle it for us."

"I mean... I think after that, it's both of you."

We all laugh until it falls silent and then Rowan stands. He slips his hands underneath me, picking me up. I wrap my hands around his neck in response.

"What are we doing?"

"Shower." He nods to the bathroom.

Finn follows, climbing into the shower to turn on the hot

water for a moment before he joins us in front of the mirror. Rowan lets my legs go slowly and my feet hit the ground. He nudges me forward against the counter and they both move behind me.

"See..." Rowan's hand slaps my ass playfully. "Just like this."

"Just like this..." I grin, staring at the two of them beside me. I'm luckier than I could have ever imagined when I see it reflected back at me like this. That these two men consider me theirs. That we trust each other enough to do all the things we've done in the last week. I just hope when they find out the truth—that I belong to them both for good—it's in kind. I have hope where Finn is concerned, but Rowan still makes my heart nervous.

Twenty-Four

R owan

"So now that we've given most of the paintings away to your anonymous courier friend, what do we do with the one we have left? How do we get it sold?" I glare at Charlotte impatiently, and she gives me a pointed look. We've been at this for an hour now.

"It's a process. I need the money just as much as you do, Rowan."

"I've got guys I need to pay at the start of the month. They'll be looking for paychecks to make the games go our way, and if I can't deliver, they won't either. Then they're likely to start talking about the situation to people we haven't paid off, and then I'll have a fucking mess on my hands. We'll all go down. You realize that, right?"

"I'm well aware. If you remember I'm on a timeline to save my brother.""

"Get off her back, Rowan. She's the one who got us this far in the first place." Hudson intervenes on her behalf, giving me a look that I don't fucking care for. Like I'm disappointing him somehow instead of the other way around.

"She's the one who got in the way of us getting the paintings in the first place." I look at her and then turn on him. "Because you didn't do your research."

"Okay. This isn't even remotely fucking productive," Finn interrupts our staring match, and Charlotte gives him a soft look that makes me want to toss a fucking table.

"Yes. Less arguing and more problem-solving. Let's just spitball ideas." Charlotte looks at me sympathetically, a new thing she tries to do to calm my temper. One that almost works until I remember she's the one pushing me to the edge with secrets.

"Tell your secret courier to hurry the fuck up. I would if I could, but since you won't let me know their name..." I throw my hands up.

"I told you what the deal was if we chose to go this route. I've always made good on my promises and never given you any reason to doubt me."

"The courier on the other hand, I neither know nor trust, and I just gave them everything of value in my possession and all the evidence they'll need to put all of us in jail."

"I trust them. I vouch for them. Do you trust me or not?" Charlotte's well and truly riled now. I can tell by the brightness of her green eyes. The way she holds mine with an unflinching challenge.

"I don't trust anyone. But I believe you."

"Then believe me when I say they'll get the paintings sold. But it'll take time. It's better this way—a sudden influx of cash that you have to launder and account for? You don't want that."

"I don't want a lot of things I have to put up with." I kick my feet back on the table and lean against the back of the chair. Finn gives me a subtle look that warns me I'm treading dangerously, but I don't know that I give a flying fuck.

This right here, this entire situation, is our lives on the line. I'm responsible for all of us. For being the wise one. The one who puts us on the right track and keeps us there, especially when we do things like this. The weight of it all is sitting heavily on my fucking shoulders, making me pissed as all fucking hell, and I can't seem to stop directing my anger at them—*at her*. Because if this goes wrong, or even if it goes right, I have every reason to think she's going to bolt afterward. A thing that'll crush Finn and judging by the way Hudson's been acting lately, him too. I'll be left to pick up the pieces, and I don't know if I'll be able to when the time comes. And that's all assuming things go well.

When I focus back on the conversation, Hudson's talking.

"They're friends of my grandparents. He's a collector of medieval art. Used to go to every auction under the sun it seemed because my grandparents would go with him, and when I was younger—and my parents were summering or skiing or whatever the fuck they did all the time—I'd be with my grandparents, and I'd have to go."

"So there's a chance he might want it—might be interested in buying it."

"A chance... but how do we even get him to meet or look at it? I can't just call him up and say, 'Hey, want to buy this painting?' That would be fucking weird and out of the blue."

"Could your grandparents warm up the conversation for you? You talk to them about it... walk them around to their friend who collects. Ask some questions out of curiosity." Finn shrugs.

"Yeah. What if you pretend like you have questions about it and are looking for someone to help answer them?" Charlotte looks hopeful suddenly.

"That could work... Maybe. I mean it's a start. But without being out there... I don't know how we show him it or bring up the conversation subtly. It's an awkward long-distance call."

"Can you go out there?" I ask.

"Technically? Yeah. My relationship with my grandparents is still good. They'd probably be happy to see me, and we have the break right now. But with hockey, I don't know how I get away."

"An injury," I suggest.

"You gonna lose your goalie right now? You remember I'm kind of pivotal to you losing and winning games, right?" Hudson gives me a look.

"Yeah, I fucking know. I mean like a temporary one. A sprain or a strain. Something that you have to get evaluated for, have some rest days. Maybe you decide to go home for a second opinion. Buys you a few days up with your family. We can make do without you for one game."

"Yeah. Okay." Hudson tilts his head back and forth.

"Sounds workable..." Finn nods along.

"Just one thing..." Hudson shakes his head. "How the hell did I come into possession of a medieval painting worth 30K? My grandparents know I have a draining bank account. That I play hockey and have zero funds to show for it. Never shown interest in art before. They're going to be suspicious."

"Fuck!" I kick back off the table, tilting my chair onto its back legs, and close my eyes. "Can you just say you won it in a poker game or something? Don't you rich kids do shit like that?"

"I'd have to have money to enter a high-dollar poker game, and we're not exactly at Yale here with a bunch of other wealthy heirs." Hudson shakes his head.

"What if it's mine?" Charlotte asks.

"What do you mean, what if it's yours?" Finn puzzles at her. "Like you gifted it to him?"

"No, but maybe I inherited it. And maybe I'm looking to sell it because I'm running out of money too."

"And Hudson's just helping you out of the goodness of his little fucking heart?" I raise a brow at Charlotte.

"No. He's my boyfriend," Charlotte says it matter-of-factly, and Hudson's brows raise, and his eyes light.

"Oh yeah?" Hudson grins.

"Hush you." She elbows him, grinning before she turns back to me. "I'm his girlfriend he met here. Maybe another down-and-out discarded heir with not much money. Maybe the painting was left to me by a rich aunt or uncle. But I need the money more than I need the painting. Hudson wants to help me and remembers his family friends back home."

Her proposal isn't awful. Not at its core. But her pretending to be Hudson's girlfriend? I don't like it. The two of them running off alone together to visit his family.

"And I want to introduce her to the only family I still like—my grandparents. I do like them, but they'll also eat that up. Especially my grandmother." Hudson looks at her but his eyes land on her hair. "But we'll have to change a few things. Lose the violet and get you some clothes that make you look like you run with their crowd. Then you'd fit right in, Duchess."

There's another exchange of grins between them, like two co-conspirators who are only too excited to head off to some secret retreat together.

"What about your real fucking girlfriend? Doesn't she live up there?" I don't like how excited he's getting about this, at all. I've suspected for a long minute that Hudson wants to be more than just Charlotte's friend. That he's been working the friend zone like he's trying to finesse his way into the goal, and it pisses me off. I'd rather he just says he wants to fuck her and be done with it. Fuck knows he loved watching her get railed by Finn and me.

Hudson sits back then, looking uncomfortable. "I don't know... I could talk to her about it."

"The fuck you will. No one is in on any of this except the four of us. You hear me?" I look at Hudson as I rock back again.

"I hear you." His jaw tightens. He's never liked the fact that I'm the boss around here. We might be good friends, but that part of his upbringing, the one that doesn't want to bow down to anyone else—especially someone without money or a family name —still revolts at the idea of listening to me.

"Good."

"Does she even have to know you're in town? I thought she lived in another city anyway?" Finn asks.

"Yeah. I could go without seeing her. I'd feel like a dick, but it's possible. My grandparents don't pay close attention to my dating life, so they wouldn't know the difference."

"Okay. So let's not overcomplicate it then." Finn's calm and collected as always. "You guys go up there as a couple. Hudson skips seeing or telling his girlfriend. There's no reason he should run into her anyway, and then the two of you can play like you're together for the grandparents. Easy enough."

Charlotte and Hudson nod along like it's a reasonable solution.

"Fine. Just don't fuck it up. We need this painting sold. If you can go out there this weekend—before the new year—get it done." My chair lands back on all four legs with a thud, and I leave the room. I don't need to see the two of them giggling about getting to take a trip together.

Twenty-Five

C harlotte

When Hudson and I arrive at his grandparents' house, I nearly choke on my own tongue. The place is a gated mansion on a sprawling property with a long driveway. The house is surrounded by a tidy front lawn with a forest bordering the outer edges. It looks like it could be a modern fairytale castle tucked away in the woods. With the snow gently falling around it, it looks like it only needs a glass globe to be the perfect little fantasy.

"I'm sorry. You're related to these people?" I stare at Hudson from the passenger seat as he puts the car in park. It's a rhetorical question really. I know the answer, but all this doesn't compute with the guy I know. Other than the fancy clothes, he's a pretty humble laid-back guy, if not a little too good at making new friends and chatting people up. I suppose that comes from a life-time of learning to make small talk at charity events and golf clubs.

He shrugs. "My dad's parents. Yeah."

"And you don't speak to your dad, but you speak to them?"

"Yes. They weren't involved in my dad's scheme, and they always hated my stepmother as much as I did, so... we make it work."

"Does your mother still live up here?"

"No. She moved to California a long time ago. I still visit her occasionally, but once she and my dad were done, she took the money and ran. I don't blame her."

"You didn't go with her?"

"No. I was young and stupid at the time. Thought my dad was a god. He seemed like he was. All the money and famous people who flowed through our house. It wasn't until I got older that I realized who he really was. That there was something that didn't make sense about how the two of them were making money."

"And your stepmom talked him into it all, or what?"

"Nah. I'm positive she contributed to it. But he was a greedy asshole all on his own. She just helped grease things for him because she knew so many people."

"Do your grandparents still talk to him?"

"I think they send him money and letters for the holidays. But they'd rather pretend their son wasn't locked up, so they mostly act like he doesn't exist anymore. Focus on their respectable children."

"Do you count?"

"I'm... a mixed bag, I think. I remind them of him. We look a little alike. I'm his only son. But they know I didn't have anything to do with it, and they've always been good to me."

"Gotcha. But be on my best behavior."

"Yeah. No pointing guns at anyone this weekend, okay?"

We both laugh, and I punch him in the arm.

"I think I can refrain from putting a gun to your grandfather's head. I mean unless he pulls some Rowan shit. Then I can't be helped."

"Nah. Nothing like Rowan. Pretty decent for a rich old guy.

He just likes playing golf and having his whiskey while he reads the financial news at night."

"Fair enough." I stare up at the house as we get out of the car and pull the wool coat I have on a little tighter around me. Hudson walks around and pulls our suitcases out of the trunk, placing one of them in front of me. One that's way too huge for what's supposed to be a weekend trip but contains all of the clothes, makeup, and hair stuff I need to look like I fit in here. Enough to make me look like I might have a wealthy great aunt who passed away and left a painting like this to me.

Hudson took me on a quick shopping trip before we came here. Apparently, my wardrobe, which consisted mostly of jeans and tees with a few dressier items for when I had volunteer activities and cute tops for going out, wasn't going to cut it for a weekend at his grandparents. So I bought two new dresses, a pair of pants and a couple of tops, this coat, and two pairs of shoes. It felt a little ridiculous, but Hudson assured me it was necessary. He sat patiently with me while I picked things out and tried them all on, giving me the thumbs up on things he thought would work best. Then we went to get burgers and fries while he gave me a brief overview of his childhood growing up. All the details of which I was trying to quickly test myself on again with mental flashcards.

———

Late that afternoon, after I met his grandparents and we had cake and coffee, we head over to his family friend's house. Hudson's grandfather spoke to him on our behalf earlier in the week and he told us to stop by when we were in town. Rolling down their driveway after we enter the gate, I feel like I'm having déjà vu. Only this time the house is even bigger, and the grounds are even more expansive than the place we just left. A wide swath of snow rolls over the front lawn, decorating the trees like it's been painted there.

"Jesus Christ. Why did you leave all this again?"

"To play hockey and get away from all the bullshit."

"Right." I forget sometimes that Hudson has his own damage. He handles it so much better than the rest of us, but it doesn't make it any less painful for him.

"Yeah," he says softly in return.

I don't point out the obvious. That now we're here doing this which is also illegal and potentially fucking over a family friend. Not that they know it. The painting is real. They just won't know we stole it instead of inherited it. But hopefully if it ever comes to that, they'll have ignorance as a defense.

"I'm sorry. It must have been hard to leave all of this."

"Not really. Seeing how people reacted. Treating me like shit just for being his kid, I was ready to leave. I wanted to play hockey instead of work in finance anyway. So, just one of those situations where it is what it is."

"But you had to leave your girlfriend behind too."

"Truth be told, Duchess; I don't know if she is my girlfriend anymore. She barely speaks to me and won't answer half my texts and calls."

"Why?"

"I don't know."

"You haven't asked her?"

"And sound like some pathetic fucking loser begging for crumbs?" His irritated tone is surprising. I'm used to it from Rowan, but Hudson's normally not so abrasive. I go silent in the wake.

"Sorry. I'm not trying to be a dick. It's just a sore subject."

"Why stay with her then? You know some of the girls on campus are dying to be with you."

"Are they?" His brow rises and falls as he puts the car in park.

"From everything I've heard."

I don't press the issue further. Whatever is lurking under the surface of all of this with him is more than I know what to do with. And definitely more than I can sort out in the time we have here together in between trying to get this painting sold and playing the adoring couple in front of his relatives.

We make the long walk up to the front door, and Hudson presses the bell. There's no immediate answer, and I rub my hands together, blowing my breath between them to try to stay warm. He presses the button again, and we wait. A few more minutes and nothing. My stomach turns. This was our only shot. The only chance we have in hell of getting the money in any sort of rapid order without a massive risk on our part.

As a last resort he grabs the large brass knocker and bangs it against the door, a little louder than is probably polite, and a voice on the other side shouts through it.

"Yeah. Yeah. Yeah. I'm fucking coming!"

I raise my brows and look at Hudson. The door swings open a moment later and a well-dressed attractive guy with styled wavy blond hair about our age stands in the door frame, a flask in his hand. He steps out.

"Hudson!"

"Ed!"

The two of them greet each other and exchange a handshake that turns into a half hug as Ed pulls the door shut behind him again.

"What the hell are you doing up this way? And here of all places?" Ed's brow furrows as he studies Hudson.

"I was going to meet with your grandfather. Have a painting I want to show him."

"A painting?"

"Yeah. My grandparents set it up with him. This is Charlotte." Hudson nods to me.

"Nice to meet you, Charlotte." Ed takes my hand, studying me as he shakes it. His face is unreadable, a practiced look of amused disinterest, so I have no idea if I'm passing muster or not.

"Is your grandfather home?"

"Oh. He's home. You don't want to talk to him right now though. We just had it out over a whole bunch of things, and he's in his office swigging scotch and muttering about how much he hates our generation. Not a good time."

"What did you do now?"

"What haven't I done?" Ed smirks.

"I won't ask then."

"Good idea."

"So no chance of talking with him at all today?"

"No. He might settle down tomorrow, but you won't get anything out of him today. And their maid is out with the flu, so there's not even anyone to serve you a drink while you wait. Just bad timing all around I'm afraid."

"Tomorrow's New Year though, and then we're headed back."

"Oh yeah. Hockey to play I imagine?"

"Right. I'm out right now with a minor injury. Only reason I had a chance to come up here for the holiday in the first place."

"Ah. Well, maybe on your way out of town tomorrow. But hey, since you're here I'm having a huge party tonight at my place. I've got a loft downtown. Gonna be packed. Lots of familiar faces," Ed offers before his eyes turn on me. "Would love to have you both."

"Uh..." Hudson hesitates.

"We'll be there. What time?" I answer because if we can't get to the grandfather maybe we can at least meet someone else worthwhile. Maybe Ed can help us get in with his grandfather tomorrow. I really have no idea, but I'm desperate to not leave here without results. I don't have time to wait on the courier or for a future chance to come up here. I need the money now, and so do the guys.

"You can head by around 10. Your number still the same, Hudson?"

Hudson nods.

"Perfect. I'll text you the address. Can't wait to catch up some." Ed's eyes flicker between us, and he takes a swig from his flask before he heads down the steps.

———

"I don't think you know what you signed yourself up for."
Hudson leans against the front desk as we wait for the clerk to
sign us in at the hotel.

"What do you mean?"

"All these rich assholes partying. Drunk and stupid. They get
wild. You're not going to like it."

"I've survived Rowan's parties."

"These are worse."

"Worse?"

"Well... I guess different and not necessarily worse. But you're
going to have to wear that dress we brought that you weren't sure
about."

I raise a brow at him. It was a tight lavish little dress that
hugged all of my curves and made me feel gorgeous and self-
conscious about things all at the same time. He insisted on buying
it. Told me I'd find something to wear it for even if I didn't need it
on the trip.

"Am I?"

"Yeah. And then I'm gonna brag to Rowan and Finn that I
got to see you in it."

"That'll go over well."

"I'll enjoy every fucking second of it."

A few moments later she returns with our keycards and hands
them to us, giving us instructions on how to get to our room and
thanking Hudson for staying with them. She assures him our
luggage will be sent up shortly along with some champagne. I
smirk as we ride up the elevator.

"What?"

"Nothing. Just that you're so different here. All charm and
manners. So fancy. Interesting to see a different side of you than
what you're like back home."

"Home, eh? That mean you're staying after this?"

"I don't know what I'm doing. I suppose a lot of that depends on Rowan and I not killing each other first."

"You've been doing better lately. I assume the détente you've all worked out is still going well?"

"Hudson…" I sigh. A flash of him in the room with us comes back to my mind, and I have to look down at the floor before my cheeks color. I loved that night. But we haven't talked about it since and I don't want to make it awkward. Especially not when we have a job to do.

"I'm just teasing. I don't mean anything. You know that right? I'd never judge you," he explains quickly, but before I can respond the bell dings, and the doors open to our floor, and a group is waiting their turn to get on the elevator.

We dodge around them and walk to our room. He opens the door, and the place is massive. It's a gorgeous suite with a small living area, a bedroom, and a bathroom so big I might get lost in it. I set my purse down and spin around, my eyes catching on a massive bouquet of fresh purple flowers.

"Oh my god," I whisper, and I reach out to touch one of the leaves, leaning over to smell them as the scent wafts through the air.

"You like them?" He walks up behind me.

At first, I thought they came with the room, but when my eyes meet his, I realize he got them for me.

"They're gorgeous. You didn't have to do that."

"Well, when you dyed the purple out to come here and made that comment about losing the good luck the color gives you, I thought we'd better make sure you still have it somewhere." He grins at me.

I jump up and wrap my arms around him. He catches me and hugs me tight.

"Thank you. This is so sweet of you. You didn't have to do that."

"I wanted to." His grin fades a little as he watches me, and there's something in his eyes I can't quite read as he sets me back down on my feet.

"Well… thank you. So much. I love them. Hopefully, they give us some last-minute luck. Seems like we need it."

"Let's hope." His eyes drift over me for a moment and then snap back up to mine. "You better get ready for the party. We can grab some dinner before we head over."

Like it's perfectly timed, there's a knock at the door, and the staff have arrived with our luggage. We both go our separate ways, and I start getting ready for our night out, still hoping somehow, we can pull this thing off without a disaster.

Twenty-Six

udson

The party Ed has invited us to is massive. It's crawling with faces I recognize but even more that I don't. The music is loud and despite the sprawling size of the place, it feels cramped; bodies and drinks flowing through the room like one undulating mass. My hand laces with Charlotte's as we cross the room, not wanting to lose her in the crowd.

That's when I see *her* across the room—my girl. My Sophia. She's standing with another guy looking like they're together, and I feel a twist in my gut. I watch her for a moment because maybe there's a perfectly good reason for this. Something that makes a lot of sense, like she's also here faking a relationship with someone because she's trying to sell a painting to pay off all the illegal debts mounting against her and her friends.

It's possible. Or at least it would have been until he kisses her in a way that makes it absolutely clear that it's not the first time the two of them are doing it. She practically climbs him when he kisses her harder. Which is also rich considering she always told me she hated PDA of any kind. That it was beneath our class.

"Hudson?" Charlotte's voice breaks through the fog.

I snap back out of my daze, trying to make it look like I wasn't just getting punched in the gut. Sophia and I have been rocky for a while. I'd definitely fantasized about other women. Mostly the one currently at my side. But I would have never in a million years touched someone else while we were still together.

"Yeah?" I try to erase my frown but it's fighting me. I feel like a fucking loser, and Charlotte's about to find out just how much of one, which makes it that much worse.

"What's wrong? You look like you've seen a ghost or something." Her hand wraps around my forearm.

"I just saw my girlfriend."

"Oh! Shit." She yanks her hand back. "I'm sorry. Is she pissed? Can we explain? I know Rowan said that we can't tell her, but we can tell her something. You know?"

I shake my head and then nod to where she's got her tongue down the other guy's throat. "No need. That's her."

"What?" Charlotte's immediately angry on my behalf which is gratifying.

"Guess I *don't* have a girlfriend and haven't gotten the memo yet."

"What a bitch!" Charlotte looks between us again.

"Now I get to have an awkward conversation." I start across the room.

"Well, I'm right here if you need me." She intertwines our arms, her elbow settling in the crook of mine.

"Thanks." I give her half a smile as we cross the room.

"Hey Soph!" I say in a bright tone. One that causes her to jump and release the guy who's with her.

"Uh... hi." She blinks, trying to make sense of my presence in front of her. "When did you get here? I didn't know you were going to be in town."

"Obviously." I give her a false smile, and her nose scrunches and her eyes darken in response.

"Well..." She looks at the guy standing next to her and then back at me and Charlotte. "Looks like we've both moved on, so I guess no need for discussions, right?"

"Guess not." I pause for a moment for her to say anything at all about the last few years or even just introduce me to the guy she's been cheating on me with, but she does neither. The guy she's with just gives me a smarmy grin and wraps his arm around her shoulder like he's an extra in a movie about sleazy assholes.

"Thank you," Charlotte says suddenly.

"For what?" Sophia looks at her, her brow knitting together in annoyance and confusion.

"For making this so easy and keeping him available for me. He's the best guy I've ever known. And with his body and being on the team? Every girl on campus has been dying to get their hands on him. If he hadn't been in a relationship at first, I'm sure he would have been taken a long time ago." Charlotte let's go of me long enough to run her hand over my chest and smile up at me adoringly. I'm going to owe her for this.

"Whatever." Sophia rolls her eyes, glancing at me for half a second before she settles back against her new guy. The more I watch them together the more I realize it's not jealousy but embarrassment that's twisting my gut. But it makes me want to get out of here all the same.

"Have a great night." I wrap my hand around Charlotte's, and we walk back across the room together.

I grab us a couple more drinks, and we settle back against the wall. I feel sick that I ever thought the long-distance thing could work. Awful that I put so much effort into her and what I thought would be our future only to have it end like this.

"We just need to find Ed and then we can leave." I shake my head and look back to see Sophia making out with her new guy again.

"Okay but kiss me first."

"What?" I look at Charlotte in confusion.

"Kiss me. If we were really together now that you're in the clear with your ex, you'd probably kiss me—right? Don't let her win."

Charlotte's looking up at me wide-eyed and leaning into my body, her hand running up my chest again, and fuck... I want her. I've wanted her since I saw her the first night and more every day since then. I sure as fuck don't want to give away an opportunity to kiss her. Even if the circumstances are terrible, I'll take it.

So I lean in, cupping her cheek with one hand while I lean down to press my lips against hers. I'm tentative and careful. As much as I want this to be real, it's not, and I don't want to take advantage of her doing me a favor. But when our lips meet, she kisses me back with a kind of tenderness and heat that makes it feel real. Especially when she reaches up to wrap an arm around my neck, pulls me closer, and presses her sweet curves up against me like she can't get enough. My heart rate kicks up in response, and my fingers slide down her spine. She kisses me like she wants me. Like she'd steal me away and fuck me senseless if she was given the chance. When we finally come up for air, my heart is beating like I've jumped out of a plane and her eyes are studying me like she's discovered something for the first time—something she likes. But they shutter a moment later, so fast I almost think I imagined it.

"That should convince her." She smiles and takes a sip of her drink. "And she is an awful person by the way. You are amazing. And probably the last guy I know who deserves to be treated like that."

"Thanks. Let's get a couple more drinks and say goodnight to Ed, then we can call this whole nightmare of a trip good, yeah?" She nods, and I finish downing my drink before ordering another from the bartender.

———

A little while later when Ed comes around, I'm already feeling the top shelf buzz. So good it's enough to make me forget most of my problems in the moment.

"I see you're having a good time." He laughs and pats me on the back.

"Kind of a disaster really. Didn't get to see much of my grandparents. Didn't get to meet with your grandad at all, and I was hoping he'd be interested in buying the painting. And then everything just goes to shit with my girl."

"With Charlotte? She looks happy enough." Ed's eyes drift to where she is across the room, laughing and taking a sip of her drink. Charlotte's found a girl her speed here, and they've been chatting for the last twenty minutes while we waited for Ed. I stupidly forgot that he thinks Sophia and I were over already. Works out in my favor, I guess.

"Yeah. She's just upset about the painting. It's her painting you know; she's from a wealthy family, but her mom was poor and when her parents divorced, she kind of got tossed aside too. Her aunt left her the painting so she could sell it, and now I can't even help her do that." I try to recover.

"Ah well that's terrible. I'm sorry." He looks at me with pity.

"It's fine. I see Soph has moved on to more interesting characters." My eyes slide back to her, and she's laughing hard at something her friend is saying.

"Yeah. New money. His dad's in tech or some shit. Thinks he's hot shit and constantly rambling about whatever six figure car purchase he's just made. Hate the guy but Soph's still close with the girls you know. So we have to tolerate it."

"Yeah. I get it."

"Your new girl seems like an upgrade."

"She is. She's... fucking amazing honestly. Never met anyone like her before. Surprises me constantly. And she doesn't care about the superficial shit like Soph did."

"Good for you. Thinking of keeping her?"

"If she'll have me. I imagine if I keep disappointing her, she'll find some other lucky bastard to take my place."

"Fuck. I'll buy it." Ed shrugs.

"What?"

"The painting. I'll just gift it to the old man for a late Christmas present or an early birthday. Or fuck, if he stays pissed at me, I'll just use it as a dartboard and send him photos."

"Don't tell her that last part." I eye him warily.

"What does she care if she has the money?"

"She's into art. Hurts her to part with it, but she needs the money more, you know? And again... I suck for not being able to help her out."

"You will when you get that big hockey contract. I have every faith." Ed gives me a genuine smile, and I smile in return, almost to the point of tears because it's another reminder of a thing I couldn't live up to. "In the meantime... Let's get you in good with your girl, okay?"

"If you're sure."

"Of course. I know you're headed back soon. Can I pick up the painting in the morning?"

"I'll do you one better. If you can wire transfer the money tonight, I can drop it off in the morning on the way out of town."

"Works for me."

"Perfect."

I can't believe my luck, but I just try to stay calm while he does some magic on his phone. He talks some more shit about his grandfather and his life, asking me for my bank numbers and some other information while he texts with his accountant. I try to keep up with what he's saying while I just watch what's happening in disbelief. It doesn't feel like this is real. That after everything, I might finally have a streak of the most unimaginably good luck.

A few minutes later, he looks up. "All right. Wire transfer should go through first thing in the morning. Now go tell your girl, so you can enjoy the rest of the night."

"Thanks, man. You're a fucking lifesaver. Honestly." I grin at him, half thrilled and half feeling like an asshole for selling him a stolen painting. The dirty work I do for Rowan doesn't usually involve directly fucking over someone I've known most of my life.

"Anytime."

"I think I'm probably gonna do the rounds and head out, but I'll see you in the morning."

"See you then."

I make my way over to Charlotte a few minutes later, trying to seem calm and not like we've just hit the lottery. When she and her new friend finally stop talking, I turn to her, using my body to shield her from the crowd and make sure no one can hear what I'm about to say.

"We did it."

"Did what?" she asks.

"Sold the painting."

"What are you talking about? How much have you had to drink?"

"A lot but that's not the point. It's Ed... We were talking, and he was just like 'I'll buy it.' Said he'd give it to his grandfather as a present or something. That easy."

"Does he have the money?"

"He paid for this party, so yeah, I think he has the money. Plus, he already initiated the wire transfer to my bank account."

"That's... insane." She looks up at me wide-eyed.

"Yes, and I need you to act happy but like... You just sold your aunt's painting happy, not we just got away with selling a stolen painting happy."

She laughs. "I'll try to control myself."

"Going to be a struggle, I know." I grin at her.

"That's seriously amazing. You saved our asses. Rowan was going to be furious and now we actually will have something to show for it." She takes a deep breath and lets it out on an exhale. "I think you might be my hero, Hudson."

And fuck do I want to be this girl's hero. Tonight and every other night that I can be.

Twenty-Seven

Charlotte

Hudson takes another long chug from the bottle and falls back on the bed.

"Cheers to being a fuckin' loser."

He was in an incredibly good mood as we left the party, but it's dimmed since we returned to the hotel. I don't know if it's the alcohol, Sophia, the fact that we're leaving tomorrow, or some combination of the above.

"You're not a loser, Hudson." I shake my head, stepping out of my heels and crawling onto the bed next to him.

I take the bottle out of his hands and put it on my nightstand. At least if it's farther out of reach for him, he might actually slow down. I can deal with funny and talkative Hudson, wild and weird Hudson, even the very strange suave old money Hudson who I'd witnessed on this trip. But drunk and sad Hudson might outmaneuver me.

He turns on his side, crooking his elbow and leaning on his

hand as his eyes dance with the drink. He looks me up and down and then meets my eyes again.

"How do you figure? I just lost my girlfriend. I have no real family who wants me. I fucking ran off to play hockey, and I'm not even good enough to make the cut for the pros. Then I fuck over a childhood friend because I need the money so badly. Now what? I go try to do something with a fucking media degree and charm?"

"Charm gets people a lot of places. You have it in spades. It's why your friend gave you the money. And I wouldn't feel bad. The party he threw tonight probably cost as much as that painting. It's not like he's worried about the money. Also... I get that you're friends, or at least friends in the way people in your sort of society are, and I know that's uncomfortable. But you saved us tonight because of it. Rowan or Finn couldn't have done that. Don't underestimate yourself."

He gives me a saccharine smile that flattens.

"Which reminds me. I'm even fucking odd man out in our house."

"What are you talking about? We all love you. You're probably the favorite, frankly. If there was a blind survey, I guarantee it. Finn might lie and say it's me if he knows I get to see, but it's definitely you if he's honest."

"I'm the one who lays in bed at night listening to the rest of you fuck."

"Oh. That."

"Yeah. *That.* Know how awkward it is for us all to be hanging out one minute, watching a movie, doing our thing, and then the three of you run off to fuck? And I have to go to bed alone. Listen to you through the walls. Cock hard and desperate to fuck someone, and my girl is a million miles away. Then come to find out she's not even my girl anymore. Hasn't been for a minute, apparently."

"Well, she's a bitch for cheating on you. I can go fuck up her car or egg her house if it'll make you feel better. And seeing him, I have no idea why she's chosen him over you."

"She wanted to get fucked in a used luxury car I assume. Besides... I can't be too pissed."

"No?"

"No." He flops back against the pillow staring at the ceiling. "Cause when I jack off, I tried hard to see her face. Imagine it was her hands and her mouth. But she kept changing into you."

My heart goes stark still in my chest. It doesn't beat. I don't breathe.

"Me?"

"It's you I hear moaning so fucking loud. You smiling and curling up to watch TV in my lap on the couch. You I'm stuck here with pretending like we're old fucking lovers selling paintings together."

"I'm sorry." I don't know what to say, so I apologize instead.

"It's fine." He looks over at me, eyes glassy. "You should kiss me again though. For real this time. I want to know what's so fucking good about it that you manage to have them both so tightly wound around your little finger."

"I do not have them wound around my finger. Jesus. They do what they want whether I like it or not."

He scoffs. "Finn is all fucking in. Has been since the night at Mitchell's. Maybe before. Should have heard the way he talked about you holding us at gunpoint. Like it was the hottest shit he'd ever seen. And Rowan is too, he just wants to pretend he's not. Give the illusion that he doesn't give a fuck about anything when you and Finn are the center of his fucking gravity."

"He cares about you too. He's just fucking proud, and you challenge him in ways Finn doesn't."

"This is a lot of fucking words, Duchess, just to get out of kissing me."

"I'm not trying to get out of it."

"Sounds like it to me. Maybe you're scared though. That I'll kiss you better than both of them. Then it'll be you imagining me on the other side of the wall."

"Oh please." I roll my eyes.

He turns toward me and purses his lips, laughing and then trying to get serious enough to purse them again.

"Come on. Just one. You can do it."

"Hudson."

"Scared. Got it. No worries. I'll brag to them about it when we get home."

"Fine!" I huff.

I lean over, every intention of a quick peck on his lips. To shut him up and give him something to make him recognize he's just projecting his fantasies onto me. His sadness over his now ex-girlfriend morphing what might be some honest frustration at being left out sometimes into something more. A momentary brush of his mouth over mine though, and my body lights like he's just struck a match. Because Hudson can fucking *kiss*. I thought it before at the party but he was tentative then. Like he wasn't quite sure he wanted to kiss me. But now? Now he's all in.

He can also manhandle me because his arms wrap around me and he drags me closer, his body lining up with mine as he grabs my leg and pulls it over the top of his. I can feel him already hard underneath me, and if I'm not imagining it, it's another surprise. Hudson has a big fucking dick.

I'm learning way too many dangerous facts about Hudson in quick succession. I pull back, putting distance between us and catching my breath.

"What was that?" I say softly.

He grins this megawatt smile that melts panties around campus. I don't know what he's worried about. His ex might have been stupid enough to not wait for him, but plenty of women on campus would line up to take her place.

"You taste like cranberries."

"You taste like you've had a lot to drink."

He grins again and then slides over the bed, stretching his

body over mine to reach for the alcohol. I reach out and grab his wrist, stopping him before he can pick it up.

"That wasn't an invitation for more."

"Not for me. For you."

"No." I shake my head. "One of us needs to stay levelheaded."

"Okay." He releases the bottle, but he doesn't move away from me, settling between my thighs instead as he looks down at me.

"Hudson…" I breathe out his name.

"I should go down to the hotel bar. Find an older woman here on business. Fuck her brains out," he mumbles as his eyes drift over my face. "She can go home and brag about fucking some big dicked young athlete in between mergers. I can finally break this fucking celibacy streak."

"You should," I agree as I wrap my legs around him. My dress falls back and bunches up around my waist, exposing most of my thighs, and he looks down to study it.

"I can finally hear a woman moan who isn't you." His mouth is an inch away from my neck, and I can feel his warm breath dance over my skin. He rocks forward, his cock lining up with my clit, and I bite my lower lip when he grazes over me.

"Know it's my cock making her sound like that and not my two best friends. Because I can't touch 'our girl.'"

The way he says "our girl" twists inside my chest. A glimpse at the broken boy underneath the constant jokes and smiles.

"Hudson." I reach up and cradle his jaw, a hint of stubble there as he looks down at me. He rocks forward again, holding the pressure tight, and my clit throbs with how badly I want him. My heart's just as desperate to show him he's wanted.

He bows his head, his lips brushing over the shell of my ear with a featherlight kiss before he whispers, "Just tell me. In a world where they don't exist, do you let me in?"

"Yes," I confess, realizing when I say the word how much I want it. How much I see Hudson as mine even if he's not.

His chest rises and falls with a deep breath and then he looks away.

"I need a shower," he announces abruptly, pulling away from me.

We both sit up, and he slides to the edge of the bed.

"I do too," I admit. It's been a long day of faking it together. Stressing about whether or not we're believable as a couple. Wondering if this whole thing would blow up in our faces.

"Good. I want to watch you." He looks back over his shoulder at me, his lashes leaving his blue eyes darker than normal.

"Watch me?"

"It's the one thing I'm allowed to do, right?" There's a bitter tone to his voice, but his eyes dance with mischief all the same. "So it's what I want, for being a good fucking little soldier and doing what Rowan asked of me. What I want from you for always turning those fuck-me eyes on me."

"I have not—" I start to protest, and he tilts his head, just the slightest bit like he's silently asking me not to lie. "It was just the once," I say softly.

"When I walked in on you three and you sucked Rowan's cock while you watched me like it was mine? Yeah. I remember it. Vividly."

"So you want to watch me shower?"

"You know what I want. Unless you want me to go downstairs."

I swallow against the lump in my throat. I don't want him going anywhere. I've always respected his relationship with his ex, and never felt particularly jealous over it. It was what it was. He was off-limits. But now, the thought of him finding someone else makes my chest ache.

"No," I admit, and then I get up slowly, my fingers going to the zipper on my dress, pulling it down bit by bit as I walk to the bathroom to turn on the water in the shower. I come back out, slipping out of the dress, and tossing it over my suitcase before I look at him expectantly, nodding toward the bathroom.

He follows me in, leaning against the counter as we watch the steam start to rise. I slip my bra off and then my underwear. Looking at him when he doesn't move to take off any of his clothes.

"I don't trust myself in there."

"You're going to stay out here?"

He nods.

"The shirt at least?" I've seen Hudson shirtless enough to know that everything under the button-up he's wearing is fantasy material. I wasn't lying when I said I didn't know why his ex would choose anyone else but him.

Twenty-Eight

udson

"Undo the buttons for me. I can't handle fucking tiny buttons right now." I try to undo them, but my fingers aren't exactly dexterous at the moment. I'm drunk and tired. Too fucking busy staring at her naked fucking body to be able to focus on how buttons work.

She steps forward, and I lean back against the counter, bracing my hands there to watch her. Too afraid I'll touch her if I don't keep them occupied. Especially when I can feel her breath against my chest as she works on them, unbuttoning each one at a slow pace all the way down my chest. When she hits the bottom, she has to pull the shirt from where it's tucked into the slacks I'm wearing, and that movement creates the tiniest bit of friction on my cock. A teasing motion that makes me want more. So much more of her that I fucking want.

She undoes the last button and then pulls the shirt apart,

pushing it back over my shoulders and dragging it down my arms. It forces her to lean closer and the tips of her nipples graze over my chest.

"That's enough." It comes out harsher than I intend, and she steps back while I toss the shirt on the counter.

"Sorry," she says softly and turns toward the shower, the sway of her ass as she steps in is almost more than I can resist. A flash of her pinned against the tile while I take her from behind, listening to her moan *my* name comes unbidden, and I have to put my hands back on the counter.

She slides under the spray of water, wetting her hair, and the steam from the shower obscures enough that I feel like I can focus again. I want this. Need this really to be able to get out of this hotel room with my dignity intact. I was only half joking about going downstairs. Rejected by my ex and constantly taunted by Charlotte's existence in every single nook and crevice of my life is driving me to a cliff's edge. One that I'm worried I'm gonna fall over.

She grabs the handheld spray and runs it over the glass, clearing some of the fog there before she puts it back and stares at me. Her eyes drift over my chest and arms, nibbling on her lower lip as she studies me. There's lust in her eyes and that at least gives me some consolation.

"I knew you had a good body under all that designer stuff you wear." She smiles at me.

"You don't like my clothes?"

"They're fine. A little fancy for my taste. I'd rather see you in a T-shirt that's been washed one too many times and shrunk down to fit all those cut lines."

Explains her fascination with Finn.

"Yeah, well I like the finer things." I don't know what the fuck I'm saying. I drank too much. I want too much. I want her to *want me* way too much. I want to have something they don't. Something she craves with the same desperation.

"Do you? You spend a lot of time doing dirty work for being so fucking fancy."

"Fancy." I roll my eyes. "You sound like Rowan. I just like nice stuff. That so bad?"

"You must like dirty things too. Get bored of the fancy ones sometimes? I bet you do. The thought of someone who isn't one of your prep school princesses or some high-end heiress. Just a normal girl on her knees for you because she really wants to be."

"Doubtful they'd want me for anything other than the money." It's why I stuck things out with my ex and stayed in my family's tax bracket when I dated. Nothing would fucking hurt my ego more. Other than maybe the moment they find out there isn't much money left.

"Have you seen yourself? Or the way half the women who come to the house look at you? They've only stayed away because you're a relationship guy. Once you let them know that's over..."

"Then you get to hear *me* fucking two other people through the walls." I smirk at her.

She stares down at the tiles on the floor of the shower then, lost in her own thoughts. Ones she must not like judging by the way her brow knits together.

"You should start showering. Don't waste the water," I mutter, staring at the way the rainhead makes the water fall over her shoulders, creating rivulets of water down her body. Ones I want to run my tongue over.

She grabs her soap off the corner and puts it on the little travel-size puff she brought with her. Lathering it up and squeezing it when the bubbles start to multiply. She runs it over her skin slowly, occasionally looking up at me like she wonders if I'm getting bored of watching and will disappear. The room fills with the scent of her, and I soak it in.

I reach for my belt, and I undo it, tossing it up on the counter and then go for my pants, sliding them off next. The movement gets her attention, distracting her from her shower, and she stares at me. Her eyes dropping down over my body until they land where I'm already hard. I pull the elastic of my boxer briefs down and kick them to the side with my pants.

Her eyes go wide at the sight of my cock, and it makes my ego swell to see her look at me like that for once. She takes a step back, pulling her hair to the side and stepping under the rainfall to wash the soap off her body. I run my hand over my cock, trying to sate the need that's there with just a taste, but it's not enough. I stroke myself again, and she steps toward the glass to get a closer look while she watches me.

"Now I really don't understand," she mumbles, referencing my ex again. The last person I want to think about. Especially not when I have everything I want right in front of me.

"Touch yourself."

Her lashes lift, and her eyes meet mine. I raise my brow in a challenge, and she meets it, sliding her hand between her legs, using her fingers to slip over her clit in slow strokes. Her teeth graze over her lower lip, and she lets out a muted sound I can barely hear over the water.

I cross the space between the counter and the shower door, pressing my palm to the glass and leaning against it. I take another slow stroke of myself, watching her and using her pace to guide my own. She closes the distance between us, moving up to the glass. Just that little motion, her crossing the space to get closer makes me smirk.

"It won't take me long. I've been wound up all day with worrying about getting caught," she confesses.

"That turn you on? Getting caught?"

"I don't know." She shrugs. "The adrenaline definitely helps." She gives me a coy smile.

"Yeah, well... I've been fucking turned on all day just watching you."

"Acting like I'm one of your heiress girlfriends?"

"Acting like you're *mine*."

Her eyes shutter, and she picks up the pace of her fingers, her tongue sliding over her lip, and I follow her lead. I stroke myself a little faster, matching her like the two of us are fucking for real. I'd give anything for it right now, happily risk pissing Rowan off if it weren't for risking his ire on her in the process. She's too loyal anyway. Too in love with Finn and too enamored with Rowan to see anyone else.

"Before things got so complicated... I used to think about you. About crawling into your bed one night and telling you to pretend I was her. I wouldn't have done it. Ever. But the thought of it when I was in the shower like this..." she trails off, and I'm left with the consequences of knowing she wanted me as much as I want her. It brings me so close to the edge I can hardly stand it.

"I think about you all the time," I confess, my breath stutters when I imagine her hand instead of mine as I talk.

Her eyes open again and drift down to where I fist my cock in slow shallow strokes. Her watching me taking me that much closer.

"Come in the shower." She nods to the door and smiles a little at the accidental double entendre she just made.

"Charlotte..." I frown.

"I won't touch you. You won't touch me. Opposite sides. I just want you in here with me," she says it so innocently like she's a siren calling me to the rocks. But I follow her request, opening the door and joining her in the steam. It immediately starts to cling to my skin, making me even hotter than I was before.

She leans back against the tiles and watches me, her fingers massaging her clit and then her head tilts back, a little gasp is followed by a soft moan, and her fingers start to slow. The sound of her is all I need. Before I know it, I'm coming, imagining I'm inside her—making her make those sounds. I stroke my cock fast and hard. A thick spray hits the tile of the floor and mixes with the water swirling there as it heads for the drain.

I brace myself against the tile, trying to catch my breath. I close my eyes and lean my forehead against the cool damp stone, letting it even out before I risk a look at her. She's similarly spent, just now stepping back under the stream of water to rinse her hands. I want to beg her for a taste, but we promised no touching, so I stay rooted where I am. But I can't go on like this. Watching her but never having her.

"I'm talking to Rowan when we get back," I announce, breaking the silence.

"About what?"

"About this. About us."

"Us?" She looks at me with a tentative smile.

"I want to at least try it. I get you're loyal to them. That you have feelings for them. I respect that and your relationship with them. But I want on the inside of it. I'm tired of being fucking trapped out here where I can't touch you. Can't kiss you without it being a made-up scenario and then still feeling guilty for it."

"Me too."

"Good. Then I'm talking to Rowan."

"What if this is all just because it's something—someone—we can't have? Then once you've had me, you'll be bored and want to go back to freedom. You'll have lots of options, Hudson. I feel like you should explore them before you decide to go down a route that leads to conflict with Rowan. I'm not worth it. I promise you."

I take the shampoo bottle from her hands and pour some in my palm, running it through the wet strands of her hair and then massaging her scalp until it creates a lather. It feels safe to touch her now, like this at least.

"It killed me when you didn't go to my bed that night. I wouldn't have touched you. But I wanted to know I was your safe place in all this. That you trusted me."

"I do trust you and you are—in so many ways."

"That's all I want. You're all I want."

She leans back into my touch, and I finish massaging her scalp, letting her slip under the water to rinse when I'm done. I get soaped up myself, and she watches me, her eyes drifting over me like she's seeing things she didn't before.

"Okay. If you're sure," she says finally.

"I'm sure."

"We should hurry up and get some sleep then. Got to get that painting to Ed in the morning and get back to face our fate."

"Right. Sleep," I acknowledge.

TWENTY-NINE

R owan

Hudson, Finn, and I are stumbling into our hotel room after our road game with a bag of burgers and a mound of fries. Hudson's flight home had been delayed and the two of them had barely gotten back in town before the three of us had to leave again for a road game. We have to get back on a plane tomorrow morning to go back home, but for tonight we're stuck in this mid-grade hotel.

"This place needs a deep clean." Hudson eyes the dust on the back of the TV and the stains on the wall.

"Just because it isn't up to your bougie-ass standards. There's nothing wrong with it. Not like it's a highway motel."

"He was just spoiled on that fancy-ass trip he took with Char-lotte." Finn grins, digging into the fries and grabbing some pop we stashed away in the mini fridge. "That hotel looked gorgeous."

"Better with her in it," Hudson says absently as he grabs his burger, and Finn drops his fry and looks at me and then Hudson.

"What the fuck does that mean?" I snap, and Hudson's dark blue eyes jump up to meet mine.

"Fuck." He tosses the burger down on the table. "I meant to have this conversation once we got back. With her there."

"I don't think I like where this is headed." I glance at Finn, and he looks like he might spontaneously combust.

"Did you touch her?" His voice is low and lethal.

"I kissed her." Finn's jaw flexes and Hudson shifts. "I had to! We were faking it for people that we were a couple. Would have been fucking weird if we didn't."

"I guess..."

"That's not everything."

I feel a deep pit in the center of my stomach. For all her rough edges, Charlotte would be better off with someone like Hudson. Her problems are mostly the result of people around her and not choices she's made for herself—her brother... us. If there is someone with the ability to make that all go away, she could finally have peace. Settle down in a loft downtown, spend her days writing a dissertation on art and her evenings attending the ballet or whatever the fuck fancy people do.

Some part of me has fantasized about giving it to her. That she and Finn and I could make that happen after all this is over. But if she has Hudson, she has zero need for us. The only thing she might miss is the rough sex, and Hudson could be trained. As evidenced by the fact he was a perfectly good guy before he fell in with us and now, he's a spy, a thief, and a racketeer.

"What's everything?"

"I kissed her again in the hotel room. Told her how much I wanted her."

"And?" Finn asks. I can see the tension radiating off him. He's thinking the same thing I am.

"She's loyal to the two of you. But she let me shower with her."

"Shower with her?" I look at him skeptically.

"I might have watched her get herself off." He shrugs,

smirking a little, and I'm ready to jump over this table and wipe it off his face. Permanently. But I stay rooted in place.

Finn doesn't say anything. Just stares at Hudson like he might tear him limb from limb if he moves the wrong way. Hudson looks up, and we must both look as lethal as I feel.

"What? I've watched before. You've let me watch. Encouraged me, frankly, to watch you all fuck. What's the difference?"

"Was that all? Or is there more?" Finn presses.

"That was all. But I want more. I'm tired of being on the outside of this. I'm every bit a part of this—just as much as you are. I care about her just as much. Fuck sometimes I think I might be in love with her."

"I thought you had a fucking girlfriend."

"They broke up. He told us that." Finn raises a brow at me.

"Did you tell Charlotte all this?"

"Yes."

"And?" I ask impatiently. I want to know if he did, and then I want to know what she said.

"Like I said before, she's loyal to the two of you. Said that we'd have to talk to you. Encouraged me to find other girls to fuck it out with first."

"Have you thought about it? She's not a fucking rebound." Finn's brows are furrowed.

"I wanted her before this ended. I wanted her before you two fucked her. She was supposed to come to my room that night. Except someone had to fucking intervene." Hudson turns on me, his eyes darkening.

"I didn't have her do anything she didn't already want to. She'd been after Finn since the first night."

"I could have at least had a shot," Hudson argues.

"To cheat on your girlfriend? Just what every woman wants. To be the side piece." Finn shakes his head, calm enough now that he takes another bite of his food.

He must be satisfied that she swore fealty to us. Assume that's enough. But I don't feel that same kind of comfort. I'm still seeing a world where Hudson is everything she wants, and we get left behind.

"I would have broken up with her if I thought I had a chance with Charlotte."

At least I know my instincts aren't wrong.

"Charlotte's right. It's been a long time since you got to stick your dick in something. Maybe you should do that a few times first before you get involved with her." I lift a shoulder, trying to seem like I'm giving casual advice.

"I don't want to stick my dick in something," Hudson snaps.

"What does she want?" Finn asks.

"She seemed open to the idea. You'll have to talk with her. She might have been trying to spare my feelings or waiting to talk to you. I don't know."

"Then it's a moot point until we get back." Finn glances at the way my fist balls up on the table and gives me a look.

———

When we get back to town I can hardly wait to talk with Charlotte. I want her side of this, and I want to make sure Hudson's not lying. I don't think he would, but I also know Charlotte doesn't care about hurting my feelings. She'll be blunt as fuck with the truth, and I want to know where she stands with him.

I find her kneeling in the closet of my room. Our closet really, at this point, half of it is overrun with her shit. A thing I half-hate and half-love at the same time. She turns when she hears me come in, smiling.

"You're home."

"Yeah. I'm home," I echo, shutting and locking the door behind me.

Her eyes go to the door and then to me.

"What's wrong?"

"Hudson spilled some secrets about your trip to me and Finn."

"Oh…" She stands, a flash of guilt across her face before she steels her spine and stands. "Well, I wanted to talk with all of us there but if you guys needed to talk it through first, I guess okay."

"Yeah. Something like that. And now I want to have the kind of talk only you and I can have. No punches pulled because there's no feelings to worry about, got it?"

She nods.

"Did you fuck him?"

"No. But we got off separately together in a shower."

"That just accidentally happened? Just both suddenly in there —you wet and him hard and needing to get clean?"

She rolls her eyes.

"He was drunk. I was kind of drunk. He kissed me, and I told him he was just projecting his feelings about the girlfriend onto me. He insisted it wasn't true. That he's wanted me for longer than that."

"And you?"

"I like him, a lot. And if it wasn't for the promise I made to you, I would have fucked him that night."

"So now what? The rich boy wants you and you're done with us?"

"I never said that."

"He said he wants you. You just admitted you want to fuck him."

"He just wants to be part of this. He's part of it in every other way. But we hold him at arm's length. He has to listen to us fuck. How would you like to be on the outside like that? I doubt you'd go along with it.

"I'd find my own girl to fuck."

"Like you did when you knew Finn and I liked each other? When you'd only let him have me if you got to fuck me in the process? Because you're so jealous you can't just let him have anything for himself."

"Jealous? Remind me again, which one of us made you come first? Because it sure as fuck wasn't Finn."

"Remind me again... we can have this conversation because no feelings are involved, right?" She stares at me pointedly. The bob of her throat, when she swallows, is the only sign at all that she cares what I'm saying here.

"Don't play games," I warn her.

I can't tell her what she wants to hear. I want to. Some part of me desperately wants to, but if I do it'll break me open. Leave me vulnerable in a way I've never been. And then it'll break us. She'll run to Finn or worse yet, Hudson, and then there'll be nothing left but scorched earth.

"If you say you don't want to let Hudson in, I'll respect it. For Finn's sake."

"Have you thought at all about Finn in this? How he'll feel? He knows it's only fucking between the two of us. Hudson wants more. You gonna let him replace Finn?"

"Finn knows how I feel about him. I doubt he feels threatened, but I'll talk with him first—and of course respect whatever he wants. I told you I wanted to talk first."

"No one's fucking threatened. You couldn't find a guy better than Finn. And no fucking way Hudson fucks you the way I do."

"Then it's not a problem, is it?"

"We'll see if it's a problem for him to watch you suck my cock. See how wet it gets you and how much you need me inside you after."

"He's seen it before, and it hasn't fazed him. Then again, with the way he looks naked... why would it?" She smirks, baiting me into a fight.

I wrap my hand around her throat and push her back into the closet, kicking the door shut behind me.

"Hudson doesn't know how to treat you. Doesn't know all the dirty things you like. How to fuck you the rough way you need it."

"He could learn. He just needs some direction," she whispers as my hand tightens. Great minds think alike, and sometimes it's frightening how closely ours align.

"Ah. So you don't want to replace Finn. You want to replace me." I let go of her throat just long enough to tug her panties off and test her to make sure she's wet. She is—like always for me.

"I mean like you said, you could just find your own girl to fuck." She shrugs absently like the idea of me fucking someone else doesn't matter to her.

"Pull me out." My hand's around her throat again, and I pin her up against the back of the closet. Her hands go to my pants, working quickly until she has me in her palm and then she touches me carefully. So slow and so sweet you'd almost think she likes me.

I grab her thighs, pulling her up and pinning her against the wall while I slide inside her. Her eyes shutter, and a small moan leaves her lips when I'm all the way in. Her arms slip around my neck. We're well-practiced at this. The way we fit together. The way I know every little thing she likes. No one could replace the way I take care of her.

I kiss and suck my way down her throat as I start to fuck her up against the wall, rattling it and the door in the process—hopefully loud enough for Hudson to hear.

"Fuck. You always get so deep," she mumbles, her head going back as she lets me have what I want from her.

"I hope you fucking told him how much you beg for my cock. The way you need it."

"Ro—" My name is cut off by a moan.

"This cunt is mine. Say it."

"Rowan, please."

"Say it."

"It's yours." Her legs wrap around me, and I get as deep as I can, pushing her to her limit then grabbing her jaw.

"That's fucking right. *My own—my* property, *my* girl."

"Fuck..." she mutters.

"And no one touches what's mine without my permission. You know it because you obeyed like a good fucking girl."

Another string of curses follows as I take her deeper and faster, and her grip is so tight her fingernails dig in, each jolt of her body against the wall digs trenches into my neck. Ones I'll make sure pretty boy sees in the locker room, so he knows exactly where he fucking stands—where she stands when it comes to me.

"I hate you... Fuck I hate you so fucking much, Rowan."

"I know you do, Duchess. I hate you too."

She comes hard on my cock, moaning so loud I feel like the whole house has to hear her. She takes me with her a few moments later, and when I pull out and set her down on her feet afterward, I smirk at the state I've put her in.

I grab a fistful of her hair and tug it back, so her eyes meet mine. They're still clouded with lust and the mix of reverence and hate that she always has for me.

"You fuck him if you want to. If Finn doesn't care, then do what you want with Hudson. You want to add another lovesick puppy to your list of admirers, go for it. Just know you won't replace this—the way *I* make you feel? You'll always fucking crave me."

"It goes both ways." Her eyes darken, a threat in them.

"I know." I let her hair go but grab her jaw and kiss her one last time. "Now get out."

She saunters around me like my come isn't dripping down her legs and gives me the finger, slamming the door to the closet behind her on her way out. I lean back against the wall and slide down it because for all of my fucking bluster—I need her.

THIRTY

F inn

Later that night Charlotte knocks on my door, and I nod for her to come in. I've been half asleep in bed trying to get caught up on the first week of work for class after being on the road for our game. I'm in nothing but sweatpants after I got out of the shower and her eyes fall over my chest, as she climbs up on the bed next to me.

"Interrupting your work?" she asks.

"I can't stare at it any longer. Everything's blurring together."

"I'm sorry. I don't have to bug you if you just want to go to sleep."

"Nah. You never bug me." I give her a half smile. I want her here, but I also can guess why she is, and it's not going to be my favorite conversation we've ever had.

"Well, I came to talk to you about—"

"Hudson. I know."

"You hate the idea?"

"I don't hate it. I've talked to Hudson and Rowan about it, and there are fair points about him being on the outside of this. Feeling awkward. I know Rowan has worried for a while that it could lead to him being pissed or disloyal because it was obvious he wanted you."

"Hudson wouldn't do that to you guys. Especially not you."

"I know. I've told Rowan, but you know how he can be."

"Yes. Far too well."

"So what? You want my permission? You don't need it. You're your own person. If it makes you happy, and if it'll make him happier in this situation... I can live with it."

"I don't want you to just live with it." She sighs.

"If you want me to be happy about it... that's a difficult task, Charlotte. Rowan's my best friend and there are days I don't want to share you with him."

"Then on those days, we don't share. I'm all yours."

"Right..." I give her a look that tells her we all play by Rowan's rules, whether we want to or not.

"He can't have us all scared into submission. We have to be able to stand up to him."

"That why the walls were rattling earlier? Standing up to him?"

Her cheeks blush, and I kiss her on each one.

"I'm teasing you."

"What worries you about Hudson?"

"He could be a lot of things for you that I can never be. Functional. Sane. Rich."

"You are perfect the way you are. Plus you could be rich. We could all be rich if the paintings get sold and we invest the money right."

"Yeah. Theoretically."

"But when have I ever given you the impression that being rich matters to me?"

"Right now it might not. But when you want to settle down,

that's going to matter. When you don't want to be fencing paintings and duping rich kids out of their money and getting justice against asshole professors? Then you're going to want someone who can blend back into normalcy. That'll never be me and Rowan."

"That's part of the appeal." She grins at me.

"Now... but later... you'll want more."

"I've wanted you for what feels like forever, Finn. I have you, and I still want more. Time isn't going to change that. At least not for me. I'm also not going to suddenly crave normalcy. All of this... it's changed me. I am who I am now because of it, and I don't want to go back. I want to get my brother back this week and then I want to be here with you guys for as long as I can."

"And when does that end?"

"I don't know. I hope it never does." She leans her head against my shoulder, and I wrap my arms around her. "I don't want to do anything to hurt you."

"Hudson won't hurt me for the same reason Rowan doesn't hurt me. What we have doesn't change because you have something with them too. But be careful with Hudson. Even if you don't want to go back to normalcy, he might someday. I don't want to see you get hurt if that happens."

"I won't get hurt. I know that's possible. I saw his life back home for myself, and I know it's different than anything we can offer him here. I imagine eventually he'll want it again. The wife and the high-paying job... But for now, he's part of this. One of us."

She's not wrong. I feel for Hudson as much as anyone here. That he gave it all up to be here to play hockey. That the hockey thing didn't work out, so instead, he's running the streets with us. Him falling for her.

I brush her hair out of her face, and she smiles up at me. Her fingers wrapping around my forearm as we stare at each other for a long moment. She leans forward and kisses me. It's soft but short, and she breaks it a moment later, starting to pull away.

"I should let you get back to work."

"Just let me get like one more hour done and then I'm yours the rest of the night?"

"Okay." She smiles at me again, kissing me on the cheek and then taking off out of the room.

Thirty-One

harlotte

I knock on Hudson's door, and he calls for me to come in. He smiles at me and sets his video game controller aside, patting the spot next to him on his bed.

"Finish having uncomfortable conversations?"

"Something like that."

"And?"

"I talked to them both, and they're okay with it. I don't think they love the idea, but they're also not fighting me on it either. They want us to be happy."

Hudson gives me some side-eye.

"I doubt that's how Rowan phrased it."

"No. Rowan and I fucked, and he told me to do whatever I've got to do, but he doesn't think you can handle watching him fuck me."

"I've already seen it?" Hudson gives me a puzzled look.

"I reminded him. But... we never talked much about it. Did it bother you? I mean, at the time I didn't ask because I didn't think you had feelings for me. And given that you watched, I assumed you just liked the live-action porn. Now I feel like we have to be sure we're on the same page about it."

"No, it was fucking hot as hell. I never thought I'd be into it though, if I'm honest. I was surprised at how much I liked watching you with them. More surprised when I wanted in and couldn't stop thinking about it. It doesn't bother me that you fuck him."

"Does Finn bother you?"

"No. Doesn't bother me. But Finn makes me nervous. You like him a lot. That's obvious to all of us."

"I like you a lot too. It's just this is new, and I've known Finn for a while. And things got intense fast when I started leaning on him through all of this. With Rowan too, if I'm honest. I'm still navigating my feelings. But I care about you every bit as much as I care about them. I'm just... in love with them, honestly. I haven't told them yet—in those exact words anyway. And I think I'm falling for you too. I feel like I can tell you that 'cause I don't think it's going to cause some inner core meltdown for you or weird you out that I've said that. Or I hope it doesn't. I guess if it does, that answers that."

"Not at all. Because honestly... same. Spending that weekend with you and the time before it. I don't know. It felt like every-thing between us just fit so easily."

"Yeah. Surprisingly easily." I smile at him, and he gives me a wolfish grin in return.

"So we have the green light to fuck then?"

"Yeah."

"How does this work? Is there a signup sheet for what nights I get to take you out?"

"No," I laugh and roll my eyes. "I don't know how it works. It's new for me too."

"And if I want to fuck you tonight?" He raises a brow.

"Then you'll have to take your turn." Finn's standing in the doorway and neither of us noticed. I jump a little at his presence and then notice that Rowan is lurking behind him in the hall.

"Figure you should get the full effect before you commit to this." Rowan saunters into the room, and I lean into Hudson a little, feeling protective of him.

"Don't rush him." I glare at Rowan.

"It's fine. He's right," Hudson agrees, and I look back over my shoulder at him.

"You really don't have to. We don't have to. Rowan's just being a dick."

"Charlotte, it's fine. I want to. I told you... I like seeing you with them."

"Yeah, Duchess. He likes seeing how well you suck cock." Rowan pulls me up to my feet. "I want to see how much he loves it when he has to watch us devour this cunt."

Rowan's hands are on my jeans, unbuttoning and unzipping them. I'm getting wet already, just at the thought of having all three of them at once. But I look over my shoulder at Hudson to check in. I can't hurt him. I won't. And I won't let Rowan hurt him either. Hudson's eyes are already dark with lust though. He's too busy watching Rowan undress me to care.

"Then shirts off at least. I'm not going to be the only one naked." I smile at Finn, who smirks and then complies. He strips down to his boxer briefs. My eyes fall to where he's already hard, and I don't know how long I can last doing anything that isn't him fucking me.

Hudson tosses his shirt to the side and then I look to Rowan whose hand is already slipping under the lace of my panties, smirking like hell.

"Such a good fucking girl. Already wet like the fucking slut you are. Even after I already fucked you once today. This is why you need three of us, isn't it? You have such a greedy fucking cunt."

"Yes." It's all I manage to get out as I go for the hem of his shirt, yanking it off when he lets me. He pulls my pants and underwear off a moment later, leaving me naked for them.

"Get on the bed for me." Rowan moves us backward, but I still glance at Hudson for permission too. It's his bed after all. But he nods, making room for me next to him. "Good girl. Now lay back against the pillows and spread for me."

I move to the middle of the bed when Finn sits down on my other side, his hand brushing over my stomach and then coming up to cup one of my breasts. He runs his thumb over my nipple and then leans over to suck on it, running his teeth over it in a way that immediately sends the sensation buzzing through my body to my clit. Rowan's already taken those couple of moments to settle between my thighs and starts a torturous drag of his tongue over me. I look up at Hudson, and his hand is already running over his cock through his sweatpants while he watches.

"Kiss her neck, just under her ear. Makes her feral." Finn nods to Hudson, smirking at me when I raise a brow at him. "What? Might as well put him to good use."

Hudson's at my throat a second later, and I'm about to melt into the mattress from how good the sensation of having all three of their mouths on me at once is. I'm fairly certain life doesn't get better than this moment. It's the last thing I think before Rowan takes my clit and starts trading off between sucking and roughly dragging his tongue over me, the two counter sensations make me writhe underneath him while he holds me down with a death grip on my hips, forcing me to take everything he gives.

I'm a moaning and muttering mess, crying out for them, and begging them in turn. Finn's attentions move to my other breast while he gently pinches the nipple that's already red and wet from the way he's been nipping and sucking on me. Rowan slides two fingers in me a moment later, and it's enough now that I can't take much more.

"Yes. Please... I'm so close." I moan, my hands on the back of Finn's head, running through his hair as he pushes me to my limits, and Hudson's mouth continues to tease and suck at the crook of my neck.

Rowan tears his mouth away from me and looks up at Hudson before he barks out an order, "Get ready for her."

Hudson pulls away from me and rips off the rest of his clothes. I look to Rowan, slightly puzzled.

"I'm gonna take you to the edge, and he's gonna fuck you over it. Good?" Rowan reassures me, and I nod in return.

Rowan teases his fingers in and out of me for a few more moments while Hudson gets back on the bed. Finn lets go of my nipple and his mouth moves to mine, kissing me softly before he looks me in the eyes.

"When he's done with you. You're mine. You're getting fucked until you're exhausted tonight." Finn kisses me one last time before he pulls away from me and sits back next to Hudson.

I'm sure when my body is sore and aching in all the right places tomorrow, I'll wish I didn't ask for torture by hockey players, but right now, I'm dying for it. I glance over my shoulder at Hudson who's stroking his cock, watching Rowan as he torments me, keeping me just on the edge with his fingers.

Just when I think I can't take it anymore, Rowan stands and grabs my legs, pulling me to the edge of the bed and then turning me over to see Hudson and Finn. Both of them are naked now, there's so much muscle on display, and both of their cocks are hard for me. Rowan wraps his arm tight around my waist and puts his lips to my ear.

"Go show Hudson how tight this cunt of mine is. How well you take cock for us. Enjoy how gentle he is, because then you get me. And you know I won't be, Duchess." He slaps my ass hard, and I see Hudson jolt a little at the motion, his brow furrowing momentarily before he realizes I'm enjoying it. "Now crawl."

Thirty-Two

Hudson

I'm so hard, and it's been so fucking long since I've had real pussy and not my hand that I'm gonna come the second I'm inside her. Watching her crawl to me, her eyes clouded with lust, and every part of her body pink and marked from the way we've been teasing her is almost more than I can take.

I have to stop stroking myself, or I'll come right on my hand. When I let go, her eyes move to my cock and her tongue darts out. And in that moment the other guys fade away, and it's just me and her. The desperate look on her face as she moves to straddle me and her hand wraps around my cock, as she teases the head by sliding it over her clit.

"Fuck me, Duchess. You look so fucking good," I mutter the words. "You need my cock?"

"So much."

"Then take me."

She follows my lead immediately, sliding the tip inside at first and letting herself adjust before she takes a deep breath and slips down over me. She gasps when she's all the way in, and slides forward, her arms wrapping around me and her fingers massaging the backs of my shoulders. She starts to ride me, and I feel like I'm seeing fucking stars. She's such a tight fit, and she moves like a fucking angel on my cock.

"Holy fuck." I can barely get the curse out, I slide my hands under her ass, supporting her while she rides me. Her eyes are closed, and she's lost in the act, her head tilting back and her dark hair cascading in waves over her back.

She shifts and starts to take me faster as she chases her orgasm. She uses my shoulders for balance, her nails digging in as she holds me tight. I can already feel myself getting close.

"Fuck. I'm gonna come. It's too fucking good," I warn her while I do my best not to lose control.

"I'm close, so close," she whimpers, pulling her lower lip between her teeth.

Finn slides behind her, his mouth on her neck, and his fingers slip over her clit. It's the little push she needs because a moment later she starts to shiver her release on my cock, riding me hard as I start to come inside her, and she takes wave after wave. I catch her as she falls forward, limp from the exertion, into my arms. I kiss my way over her jaw and down her throat.

"That was so good, Hudson," she whispers, her eyes opening and lifting to mine.

"That was hot as fuck," I groan because I'm beginning to understand the sounds through the wall and why they're so possessive over her.

Her lips press against mine in a soft kiss before she pulls away from me. Finn takes her, laying her down on my pillows as he starts to kiss his way over her body and she reaches out for him, her hands drift through his hair and over his arms. It's obvious how obsessed he is with her, how much he pays attention to every reaction she has and what she wants.

"You think you can come again for us?" he asks her softly before he slides his tongue over one of her nipples.

"Yes. I can try," she answers, her eyes half open as her fingers twine through the hair at the back of his head.

"How do you want my cock, gorgeous?" He kisses her other nipple, and she arches up for him.

"Any way you want, Finn."

Just watching the two of them interact is threatening to make me hard again. Because the desperation they have for each other is fucking hot.

"You think you could take me here?" He slides his cock over her clit and teases her pussy until she writhes against him.

"Always." She nods, and he kisses her again before he slides inside. She moans for him, one of her legs tangling with his as he takes her deeper and starts to fuck her.

"Oh fuck, Charlotte. You're so tight. Your come and his... It's making you so fucking warm and wet. Fuck you're such a good girl for us. Letting us have you like this."

"I want to feel you come. Please, Finn." Her nails rake down his back as he starts to fuck her harder. Her whimpering and gasping has me running a hand over my cock again.

Finn grabs her by her hair and tilts her head back, biting and licking his way down her throat while he takes her hard and fast. She whimpers that she's close again, and his hand slides between them, massaging her clit as he fucks her. He groans loudly as he comes inside her, pulling out and letting the combination of the three of us drag over her inner thighs. She reaches out for him, and he kisses her again, slow languid kisses that make me look away for a minute. Then he lays her back against the pillows again, and she closes her eyes, catching her breath for half a minute before Rowan stands.

"You ready for me, Duchess?" Rowan's voice breaks through the fog the rest of us are in, and she sits up, blinking for a moment as her eyes drift over him, and then rolling forward onto her knees, she crawls to him.

"Look at you. So fucking obedient already." He grabs her by the throat, pulling her up and straightening her spine. "Did they fill my slut up or do you still have room for me?"

"For you." She doesn't have the same lust-filled look she had for Finn or even for me. The way she looks at him is different like she's daring him to do his worst.

His fingers dip inside her, and he holds them out for her.

"Taste," he orders.

She leans forward and takes them, sucking the tips of his fingers and then running her tongue over them like she wants every last drop of the three of us. Like she's taunting him.

"Now me." He grips the back of her neck and pulls her down, forcing her face to his cock. "Suck me, Duchess. Show them how much you crave the taste of me."

I expect her to fight him on it. The way she fights him on everything. But her eyes go soft instead. To my surprise, she takes his cock greedily. Her hand wraps around him and counters the strokes of her mouth over his head. His fingers rake through her hair and then tighten around the strands as he pushes her face down on his cock, groaning with how good she must be sucking on him.

"I want to feel your throat, Duchess. Let me have it." She moves her hand, and he pulls her down. There's a little choking sound from her, and her eyes start to water but then she pulls away for a second before trying to take him deeper again on her own. I look up to see Rowan watching me watch them.

"You've got Hudson all worried. He thinks you don't like it rough like this. He's figuring out what a little slut you are for my cock. You think he can take watching you like this?"

I roll my eyes at him, too turned on from watching her to care much about what he's saying. She pulls back though, looking over her shoulder to check on me and gives me a reassuring look. I smile at her, and she smirks when she sees I'm getting hard again. She looks back at Rowan, her palm running down his chest.

"What do you need?"

"You coming on my cock until I wear you out like my own personal whore while they watch."

"Okay." She steps down off the bed, pulling close to him and kisses his neck until he turns her around and bends her over the bed. He teases her with his fingers for a few moments and then slams inside, and she grabs a handful of the comforter.

Her breath leaves her for a moment when he takes her deeper and then she inhales another, gasping when he slams into her again. He's rough with her, grabbing her by her hair and pulling her up. Fucking her hard while she begs for him to take her harder. By the time she's close again, her face is buried in the sheets, and she's a whimpering mess.

"I can't again. I can't. I'm so close, but I can't."

"You can for me." He flips her over and hits his knees, burying his face in her pussy and sucking on her clit. He works her over until I can tell from her stuttered breaths, she's close again. She gasps and her fingers white knuckle the edge of the bed while she spreads for him, her hips countering.

"Oh my god. Fuck... Yes. Please." Her whimpering goes straight to my cock, and I see Finn have to shift next to me. "Fuck me, Rowan. Now."

He stands again, sliding inside, and bends to kiss her throat once more before he wraps his hand around it, squeezing a little then fucking her hard again.

"Fuck, you taste so fucking good when you taste like all of us, Duchess. You were made for this, made for *us*." Rowan tightens his grip, and she cries out.

They come together, a sweaty fucking mess, making sounds that have me so fucking turned on I'm going to have to jack off again later thinking about them.

Finn reaches for her a few moments later, pulling her up the bed and nestling her in between the two of us. Then Rowan lays down, resting his head on her lap. She runs her fingers through his hair and leans her head on my shoulder while Finn kisses hers.

"That was... a lot for you. Are you okay?" I ask, sweeping some of the hair out of her face.

"I'm good. Just exhausted as was promised." Her fingers brush over Rowan's temple, and his eyes close. I've never seen the man as docile as he is right now, his head in her lap like he belongs to her.

"I'm gonna run a bath for you." Finn kisses her cheek and then gets up, pulling on his sweatpants before he leaves.

"Thank you!" she calls after him, smiling as she watches him walk out.

"Is there something I can do for you?" I ask.

I feel out of my depth right now, almost a bit out of place even though we're in my room because she continues to surprise me. Some part of me had hoped that maybe this experience would ruin it for me. That seeing her with them when she'd just been with me would make me jealous or hurt. Except I loved every second, and I never felt for a moment like she didn't want me here. But I'm still learning how this works and the three of them seem to already have it figured out. It probably helps that Finn and Rowan operate like each other's other half most of the time anyway.

"No. You were perfect. As always. Are you okay?" She blinks and looks at me, sitting up a little like she's realizing she forgot to check up on me.

"I'm good."

"If you two are going to do the whole post-fuck bonding thing, I'm out." Rowan kisses her thigh and pulls away, standing and putting his clothes back on. He nods on his way out and disappears down the hall.

When he's gone, she looks back at me, her eyes running over my body like she's trying to be sure I haven't been bruised or damaged. When she looks up at me again, I lean down and kiss her, and she answers it. Her lips are soft, and the way her fingers run over my body, delicately exploring my skin. I feel like I'm some interesting piece of art she's found and is appreciating for the first time. I pull back and look at her again.

"I take back what I said before. I don't think I could fall."

"No?" Her brow furrows.

"I think I'm already getting there."

"And you're okay with them?"

"Yeah. Sometimes I get you alone though, right?"

"Sometimes for sure." She kisses my cheek. "And Hudson?"

"Yeah, Duchess?"

"I'm getting there too." She grins at me.

THIRTY-THREE

C harlotte

I sit with Hudson for a moment before I go to jump in the bath, making sure he's okay given how much has changed for him in such a short period. When I get to the bathroom in Rowan's room, he's nowhere to be found, but Finn is just finishing the bath for me. I'd thrown one of Hudson's shirts on to walk through the house—for what reason I don't know, as I obviously don't need to be modest around any of these three anymore.

"Hey." Finn's eyes go soft, and he stands when he sees me. He wraps an arm around me, pulling me close, and I lay my head against his chest. "How are you feeling?"

"Sore but good."

He kisses the top of my head and then leans over to shut the water off.

"Bath should help some, but if you need an ice pack or anything just let me know."

"Thank you. You're the best, you know?" I stand on my

tiptoes and kiss his nose. He grins at me and pulls the hem of the T-shirt up, undressing me and then holding my hand while I climb into the bath.

He sits at the edge of the tub, leaning against it, and talks with me about his day, the team, and a couple of his current art projects. He asks me a million questions about how the trip to see Hudson's family went and what Hudson's life is really like back home. We talk about all the things we're going to do once my brother's home later this week and how excited he is to meet him. His fingers interlace with mine on the edge of the tub while we talk, and my heart feels fuller than it ever has in my life. He's mid-sentence, telling me about gouache and watercolor and his latest inspiration for a landscape painting when I interrupt him.

"I love you."

His brows raise, and his eyes go wide like he's trying to process what I've just told him.

"I told Hudson already but—"

"You told Hudson you love him?" He sounds surprised.

"No. I told Hudson I love you. You and…" My eyes flick to the door, implying the man whose name I'd rather not say.

"I know you're in love with him." Finn's eyes follow mine to the door.

I frown a little. "I know it won't be returned, but that's okay. You love him and somehow you know he loves you too, right?"

"Yeah, but I'm like a brother to him. You're… way more complicated than that. I don't know that he knows what to do with you."

"He is who he is, but it's enough for me. At least as long as he's like this, where we're honest with each other about where we stand and how we treat each other. It's probably the most I can expect from him."

"As long as you know what you're doing." His fingers tighten around mine, giving me half a smile.

"Never mind about him though. Are you—I mean, you don't

have to say anything back—but are you okay with me feeling that way? Am I fucking it up by telling you?"

"Fuck, no." He shakes his head. "I've been dying to hear you say it. Wanting to tell you myself but not wanting to pressure you with everything that's been happening. I've liked you from afar for years. Wanted you like fucking crazy since that night. Now... I just love you, Charlotte. Unequivocally."

His finger swipes at the tear that's starting to fall down my cheek.

"Don't cry about it though. You'll give me a complex."

"I'm sorry... I just. Hearing you say it. I'm just so happy. And I've spent so long waiting for the next thing to go wrong, and you make me feel so safe."

He leans over the edge of the tub and kisses me.

"Of course. I have you. Always."

We sit like that for a while longer, until the water gets cold, and I need to hurry up and finish getting clean. I jump in the shower for a quick final rinse and to wash my hair. He lets me finish alone, leaving me with a towel and a kiss.

When I make my way out to the closet, Rowan's there on the bed. The black sheets are unmade, and his eyes track me as I cross the room and go to the door. I slip into PJ shorts and a tank before I come out again. He mutes the TV and nods to the spot next to him.

"What are you watching?" I look at the TV but it's on a commercial.

"Nothing really. Just waiting for you." He reaches back to his nightstand, grabs a water and a bowl, and hands them to me. "You should eat and drink. I can get you something else if you want."

I look down at the bowl, and it's full of blackberries and raspberries mixed together. My heart skips in my chest at the gesture. If it were anyone else, I'd shrug it off. I would think that maybe it was the last thing we had in the fridge or maybe he got it for himself and didn't want it. But with Rowan, it's more.

"Thank you. I love it," I say softly, keeping my eyes glued to the fruit.

"I'll eat the blackberries if you don't want them."

"I want them."

"I thought you preferred raspberries."

"Turns out I like them both. Love them both really." I risk a glance to look at him.

He shifts against the pillows before he speaks.

"Good. I love them both too."

I hold up a blackberry for him, and he takes it, grabbing the controller again to flip through the channels on the TV.

"What are we watching?" I ask.

"You pick. Just use your power wisely. And know that it means you're staying in this bed tonight."

"Okay," I grin at him and hold out my hand for the remote. He shakes his head as he hands it to me, but I don't miss the small grin that breaks free anyway.

Thirty-Four

R owan

I drive her to the meet with Steven myself. Hudson and Finn wanted to go. Finn had practically insisted on it, but I refused. If anything goes wrong here, I don't want them involved. I don't need either of them going down for this, and someone is going to have to make sure she's okay if it goes badly. I glance over at Charlotte and her knee bounces in the seat next to me.

"It'll be fine," I say calmly, wanting to reassure her and wishing I had better words. Though I'd probably scare her if I did.

"I know. I just... hate this. I just want to make sure Brady is safe. Get him back home and know he's okay. I want him to have a fresh start, and I don't trust this guy."

Her calling the place she lives with me—with us—home makes my heart skip half a beat. I reach over and run my fingers over her knee.

"None of us do. But we'll be okay." I'm driving down a dark

road to an out-of-the-way meeting spot in a forest preserve that Steven picked.

I didn't tell Charlotte, but I went there earlier this week to scope the place out. It looked abandoned like the maintenance staff haven't even been there in weeks. Which made it all the more likely that he's intending to do more than just take the money. He also told her to come alone which was never even a possibility, but we'll need to make it look like it is.

"We're almost there. I'm going to pull over and get on the floor. You can drive, make it look like it's just you. But you need anything, I'll be right here, okay?"

"Okay." She nods as I pull the car into a turnoff, and we shuffle positions. I climb into the back, sliding down and getting my legs partially under the seat. I have to scrunch down to even try to fit. The only bonus is that it's dark outside, and I doubt he'll be able to see well enough to notice even if I'm not perfectly hidden.

She starts to drive down the road again and then I feel the car turn, hitting gravel instead of pavement as she pulls into the meeting spot. There's an old outdoor restroom that he wanted to meet at.

"He's there already."

We've come a few minutes early. I hoped we could get a jump on him, but he's been several steps ahead of us at every turn.

"Park as close as you can." I want to be nearby if I need to act. I made her leave her cell phone at home, and I left mine too. No one we could call for help could get here fast enough anyway, and I don't want anything identifying on us if we run into trouble with him and have to make hard decisions. But it means there's no way but her screams that I'll know when she needs me. That makes me sick.

"Okay."

"You've got it all rehearsed in your head, Charlotte. You'll be okay. Crack the window just a tiny bit, so I can hear."

"Yep." Her voice is tight. I can hear the stress in it. Practically feel the tension rolling off her as she grabs the bag of money.

"Charlotte?" I call to her just as she goes to get out.

"Yes?" she whispers.

"You can do this."

She takes a breath and hops out of the car, shutting the door behind her. I listen as her feet crunch across the gravel, and I can feel the cool air leaking through the cracked window. I hear the two of them greeting each other, a third male voice too that I assume is her brother. That's a good sign at least.

Charlotte has more than what she owes him in the bag. We made the plan that we'd pay him a bonus in order to incentivize him to stay away for good. Pay him off essentially to stay away from Brady and from her. I imagine he wants a different mark anyway after all this trouble. But there's still that gnawing worry in my gut that since he's gotten his money once, he'll try to get it again—see Charlotte and Brady as rich targets who can deliver when he threatens.

I flex my fingers, stretching my gloves, and pat my hip to make sure my gun is still there. I hear her voice and a male one answering her. The cop doesn't bother to check the car for other people, probably just doing a cursory check from a distance to make sure he doesn't see a passenger. He's counting on her to be a dumb naïve college kid just trying to save her brother. And I'm counting on him being stupid enough to believe that—leaving her alone because she's not a threat to him. Maybe even thinking he can swindle her out of more money again in the future.

I hear the hushed tones of their voices as they talk across the way, coming through the late-night air crystal clear but barely filtering through the small crack in the window. I have to hold my breath more than once to check to make sure there are no raised voices. If I hear a scream, I want the warning that precedes it.

Another minute later, I hear a male voice call out and a female voice returns it before I hear footsteps, they're heavy across the sidewalk and even heavier and faster when they hit the gravel. Like someone's jogging. Another set follow, hard on the gravel.

My body tenses, and when I hear a hand hit the door and then struggle with it, I grab the garrote in my pocket. I ease out from my spot when I hear the heavy panting and a body hit the driver's seat, but no one speaks. She'd have said something by now. If he's done anything to her, even just left a handprint on her like he has in the past, I will fucking torture him to death.

I move quickly then, jumping to the spot behind the driver's seat and pulling the garrote around the person's throat. Just before I can pull it tight though I hear a cough. Her cough.

"Rowan!" she chokes on my name.

"Fuck!" I cry out, dropping and hopping into the passenger seat to look at her. "Are you okay? I thought you were him. The way you ran, the way you flipped the door handle."

She glares at me, jamming the keys in the ignition and turning the car on.

"Get down." I see him in the distance, his head tilting as he watches us—well aware now that she has company. I slink down in the seat even though it's useless.

A second later the back door across from me opens and a guy who looks a little younger than us jumps in.

"Rowan, Brady. Brady, Rowan." Charlotte makes quick introductions.

He nods at me, and I return it before my focus goes back to her.

"Why were you running?" I demand.

"It was a jog, not a run," she corrects, and I make a noise. "Because I took a photo of him and the money with an old digital camera I had." She holds it up and then tosses it back to Brady.

"Charlotte. Jesus, fuck. Do you want to die?" I ask, as the car moves toward the access road.

"I told him I needed it to make sure he wouldn't fuck me over. He was pissed. Called me a saucy little minx before he spat at me. Then suggested I go back to his truck to get a lesson." She's driving in reverse on the gravel like she's some kind of pro getaway driver, and I think the two of us need to talk more about her life before I met her. Between this and the gun incident the first night, I'm starting to think Charlotte was never as innocent as I thought she was.

"He fucking what? I'll fucking gut him."

"Don't worry. Brady was about to hit him. Like an idiot." She turns her ire on her brother, her eyes flashing in the rearview.

"He fucking deserves it. All of it and more." Brady says bitterly, his eyes flashing with rage. I don't doubt I would have had help tonight if I'd needed to dispose of Steve's body.

"That's why I grabbed Brady's hand and ran. Wasn't expecting to fucking get garroted when I got back to the car." She glares at me for half a second before backing onto the road and peels out. "Why didn't you tell me that you had that on you? Do you have your gun too?"

"Yes, I have my fucking gun. I needed options in case I had to kill him."

"You were going to kill him for me?" Her voice takes on a soft surprised tone, and she glances at me.

"Obviously. I was hoping he'd think you were just a dumb college kid. Then you went and had to be a smartass. Surprised you didn't put his own gun to the back of his head."

She reaches over and puts her hand on my thigh and grins.

"I only do that for you."

I can't help the smile that comes to my face, and I slip my hand over hers, covering it and then threading our fingers together. Brady clears his throat, but I tighten my grip on her, running my thumb over her.

"Fuck. I'm just glad you're okay. I was terrified he was going to hurt you."

"I'm sure it won't be the last we see of him, but at least for now I've got you back." She looks up at her brother again. "We're going to get you a fresh start. Away from him and all his bullshit. You're safe now."

He presses his lips together and nods. I'm guessing the last thing he feels yet is safe. Especially not knowing who I am or where he's headed. But she was right about him being a little like me at his age. I can see it in the defiant set of his shoulders and the wary way he watches me. He's as protective of her as she's been of him.

It's clear the two of them have probably spent a good chunk of their childhood back-to-back in these kinds of them-versus-the-world situations. I hate that I see so much of myself reflected in them. They both should have a better shot than they've had at life. Where she's concerned especially. I want to make it happen, not drag her down with me.

"We can get you both a fresh start." I hedge my bets as I glance over at Charlotte because if I have to let her go—if *we* have to let her go—I want to know sooner rather than later.

"I already have my fresh start." She looks at me, her eyes soft and she squeezes my hand with the sort of pressure that goes all the way to my tired broken heart, making it beat again.

THIRTY-FIVE

Charlotte

It's a new semester, and I'm walking down the art building hall at a breakneck pace. In part because I need to get across campus to get to my next class and in part because Colin's office is down one of the side halls, and I've been doing my best to avoid him. After the holidays were over, I broke up with him via text like a coward. If you could call it breaking up. Really more like ending the mutually exploitative situationship we'd been having—even if he will hopefully never know it was mutual.

"Charlotte, can I speak to you in my office?" Colin's voice breaks through out of nowhere, and I nearly trip I'm so startled by it. I have to keep it together, learn how to be normal around him—at least until we all graduate in a few months. I'm just hoping he thinks my anxiousness is about our going separate ways and not anything else.

"Um, I'm in a bit of a hurry to get to my next class."

"It will only take a minute."

"Can you just tell me here?"

"It'd be better if we spoke in my office."

"Like I said I have a class, so maybe another time?"

"It's urgent. I need to speak to you, *now*." My heart skips a beat in my chest. There's no way he could have found out. No way he could know it was me that did it. We were so careful.

"Okay," I whisper because if I've been found out, the last thing I want is for it to be said loud enough for the whole building to hear. I follow him down the hall to his office, and he unlocks it and motions for me to follow him in.

I hover near the door as he sets his bag down.

"You can come in and shut the door behind you." His brow knits, and his eyes search over me for a moment.

"I really am in a hurry if you could just tell me what's urgent." My heart is racing in my chest. My brain is flooding with thoughts about whether he might report me to the administration or if I'm about to go to jail. He frowns at the door and then at me, rounding his desk to get closer to me.

"Charlotte, I feel like things ended so abruptly between us. I'm sure some of that—a lot of that was my fault. I know I've been gone a lot lately and haven't always been available to you. If you're mad about that, if that's the reason for things I wish you'd just use your words rather than this childish behavior."

"Childish behavior?" I repeat, trying to make sure I heard him right and that this abrupt right turn into him being an asshole really just happened in the middle of what sounded like it was going to be an apology. Because frankly, he was an ass. If I had still liked him the way I thought I did in the beginning, this would be ruining any chance he had of a reconciliation.

"Texting me and then giving me the silent treatment *is* childish behavior."

"I'm not giving you the silent treatment. I've just moved on," I say incredulously.

"Please, Charlotte. We both know how you feel about me. That you've been doing your hardest to get more out of me than what we've been doing. And I understand that a girl your age wants a relationship. You think it's all hearts and roses. But I was clear when we started this that I'm too busy for a relationship."

"Which is fine. I'm just not interested in being that girl anymore. I'm sure you'll find someone else more age appropriate."

"Not interested anymore?" He laughs. "That's why over break you were sending me voice memos of you touching yourself?"

The urge to tell him the truth, to watch his face crumple with the realization and put his ego back into place, where it belongs, is high. But I'm not stupid enough to do that, as much as I might want to.

"I don't think this is an appropriate conversation to have here."

"You don't answer my texts, so it's been difficult to have it anywhere."

"Because she's busy." Finn interrupts, stepping into the threshold of the office.

Colin's attention jumps to him and then his eyes bounce between us. He takes a step back like suddenly I'm poisonous to him. His eyes narrow as he looks at me.

"Please tell me you're not silly enough to waste your time on someone like him?" Colin laughs halfheartedly.

I reach back and grab Finn's hand, threading our fingers together, and he squeezes mine back.

"Not wasting any time at all," I say firmly.

"Clearly," Colin scoffs.

"Just leave her alone. Don't text her anymore." Finn edges closer to me.

"Or what?" Colin stands a little taller, and I'm honestly shocked he's trying this. He's a good five inches shorter than Finn, and I have no idea how many pounds lighter. Dozens I'd imagine. I assume he thinks his status as a professor will keep him safe, but he doesn't know Finn.

"Or else I'll make sure you do." Finn takes a step toward him, and Colin raises his brow.

"This caveman thing does it for you then? I thought you were brighter than that." Colin's eyes dodge away from Finn and land hard on me.

"I love him. So yeah, the caveman thing does it for me. He can pull me around by my hair any day he wants." I tighten my grip around Finn's hand and tug. I want out of here before Colin triggers Finn's temper with all this bluster. I don't want to see him get into trouble for me. "Finn?"

Finn breaks the locked stare he has on Colin and looks at me, his face softening, and I nod to the door. He follows my lead when I give another gentle tug in that direction, and Colin lets us leave without another word. Although I somehow doubt it's the last I've heard from him.

When we've put distance between us and the professor, Finn shakes his head. "I was down the hall when I saw him approach you, and I could tell you weren't feeling it, so I followed. I can't stand him. I don't like the way he keeps pursuing you."

I run my thumb over his in reassurance as we walk to our class together.

"We're almost done here, and it'll all be behind us. All that matters now is that we've got each other. Isn't that what you tell me all the time?" I flash him a playful look.

"How dare you use my own words against me." He smiles and then leans down to kiss me before we walk into the studio together. I kiss him back and can't help the grin that comes because for once in my life, I have everything I could ever want.

Epilogue

One Year Later...

harlotte

I'm standing out by the shed grabbing a few handfuls of wood, shivering even with my coat as the snow falls around me. I'd rented this cabin up in the mountains to avoid people and get away from everything for a while. So Christmas Eve is going to be a quiet affair with cookies and mulled cider by the fireplace. I just need to get a few more logs inside so there's enough to keep it going through the night.

When I go to head inside the house, I hear a rustling sound followed by the crunch of footsteps in the snow. I whip around quickly to see a shadow just this side of the woods. A large man dressed in all black. He takes a step toward me and my heart stops in my chest. I freeze in place, willing my mind to work and glancing at the cabin. I could make it in time from here. Maybe. If my feet would work.

Like he senses my skittishness he takes another step forward and my heart skips another beat. My gloveless fingers numb from the cold as I try to flex them around the wood in my hands. I might be able to use it.

"Run!" he bellows.

My heart takes off at a million beats per minute at the sound of his voice. My feet finally cooperate and I press the firewood to my chest as I hurry toward the house. It's uphill and the snow has drifted to large wavy peaks, but I'm still hoping I can make it through.

I run as fast as my legs will take me in the heavy snow, one step after the other causing a flurry of white into the night air like an explosion of crystals sparkling against the light from the house. Every heavy breath I take forming a hoary little cloud.

I can hear him behind me; his footsteps getting closer, the sound of his heavy breathing at my back. I push myself harder, running just that little bit faster. As fast as I can go. The steps to the cabin are in reach. I can make it. So close if I just try hard enough.

My boots hit the steps and I nearly slip on the bit of ice that's there, shifting the firewood and reaching out just in time to grab the railing to steady myself. I stomp up them as fast as I can, grabbing the door handle as I hear even larger boots hit the bottom step. My heart leaps into my throat as a I struggle with it, cursing the fact that the thing was probably older than me. I manage to get it to give at the last possible second. Just as the steps hit the porch and I burst through the door, turning to slam it shut. But a large hand stops me, and I drop the wood, listening to it scatter across the floor of the cabin until my heart beats so loud I can't hear anything else.

I take a step back and then another. The living room is softly lit by the fire but I'm unfamiliar with it. I know it's only a matter of time before I run into a piece of furniture and go over backwards. I glance behind me as I take another step and when my eyes return to the doorway, he's inside. Towering in front of it, dressed in all black, a black mask and black gloves making it impossible to see anything but the gray eyes that glitter in the firelight.

I glance to the right where the steps are to the upstairs loft. The bedroom's up there and it has a small window. It'll only buy me time, but not safety.

I take another step back and an arm wraps around my waist. Another darts out to cover my mouth before I can scream—the black leather pressing tight against my lips. I look up at the man in the doorway and his chest rises and falls with laughter.

"Not fast enough, Duchess." His deep voice sends a shiver up my spine.

"You know what happens when we catch you," the man holding me silent whispers against the shell of my ear. I squirm in his arms, and it only makes him grip me tighter.

"I won't let them go too hard on you," a third voice adds from where he's seated on the couch. His blue eyes glitter and he winks at me.

I look back to Gray Eyes and he shuts the door, flicking the lock before he turns back to me and closes the distance between us down to mere inches. I take a breath trying to steady my nerves, narrowing my eyes and steeling my spine in defiance.

"Masks on or off?" The one behind me asks before he starts to pull my coat off and toss it to the side, keeping his hold around my waist with one arm. I reach up and grab the mask on the man in front of me, pulling it off and tossing it on the floor.

Rowan runs his fingers through his messy brown hair and smirks at my eagerness.

"Masks off. Gloves on." I give him a wry smile in return.

"That's a new one," Finn remarks as he tosses his on the side of the couch.

"It's Christmas. Almost." I shrug.

I toe out of my boots and socks as Finn pulls my sweater off. Rowan works on my pants while I work on his, and he turns me around to face Finn as he pulls them down my legs and sets them on top of the pile we've made on the rug. Rowan makes quick work of my bra and Finn's eyes rake over my body as I work to undo his belt and pants.

Rowan's hand slides over my chest, cupping my breast and then moving to where my heart is still racing.

"Fuck. You liked that didn't you? Are you as wet as you are breathless?" He kisses his way down my neck and his hands drift down my body. I have to force myself to focus.

"Hudson?" I ask as I turn to look at him still sitting on the couch.

He'd won the hand of cards that set this game in motion earlier in the evening which meant he got to make the decisions tonight. He's momentarily distracted and the sweet look of appreciation he gives me when his eyes meet mine makes my heart melt. I kiss Rowan and Finn and then walk over to him and climb in his lap, kissing my way down his neck as his hands slide up my thighs.

"Yes?" he finally answers when I pull away. His expression is half-distraction and half-lust.

"What do you want for Christmas?" I grin at him.

"Uh..." He pauses, smiling a little. "I can't think when you're like this. Never fucking gets old." He kisses me again and then blinks like he's trying to focus. "Remember that fantasy you had early on? The one you confessed shortly after we got together."

The knowing look he gives me makes all the heat in my body pool low.

"A secret fantasy?" I can hear the interest and amusement in Finn's voice.

"Yes," I answer, watching Hudson's expression turn mischievous.

"I was thinking here in front of the fire on Christmas. That's kind of like one of those sweet holiday movies, right?"

I laugh. "A version of it I guess."

"I think we should try it. On the rug there. It'd be perfect. Them and then me to finish you off."

"What's the fantasy?" Rowan asks.

Hudson nods for me to tell them.

"When I first ran into you all—last year at the professor's house. I had a fantasy about you fucking me face down on the ground. Taking turns."

"Oh fuck..." Finn mutters, and I can tell he loves that idea. A sound of approval from Rowan and Hudson smirks at me.

"She can suck Rowan off while you fuck her Finn. But I want to be the one that finishes her off." Hudson flashes them both a warning look and then turns to me. "And you don't get off. No touching yourself. No Finn touching you. I get to do that tonight." I nod my agreement, biting my lip when I smile. I love this side of him.

Hudson grins in return. "Good. Go."

I kneel down on the floor and wait for Rowan and Finn to finish stripping while I watch. It's a sight I will never ever get tired of—all the tattoos and muscle. Every single inch of them that still makes my heart flutter like I have a schoolgirl crush.

Rowan sits down on the floor in front of me and I lean in to kiss him. His hand wraps around the back of my neck as he kisses me roughly and I brace myself on his thighs.

"We're gonna have to do that chasing thing again Duchess. But next time I'm not giving you a head start. And when I catch you, I'm gonna fuck you right there in the snow," he whispers against my lips when we pause to catch our breath.

"I think I might need that."

"I know you do." His lips twist with amusement. "Right now I need your mouth on me though. Feel this pretty little tongue all over my cock." His thumb presses between my lips and over the tip of my tongue.

I lick my way over the pad of it and then bend down, taking him in my mouth just as I feel Finn's hands on my inner thighs. His fingers brush lightly over me and then he presses gently to get me to spread for him.

Finn leans over me, kissing his way down my spine and over my ass until he nips at my thigh and squeezes my hips.

"Love this view, Duchess." His fingers brush between my legs, testing to make sure I'm wet enough before he slides inside. A small groan of approval when he feels me clench down on him. "The way you feel though... So fucking good."

I take Rowan deeper as Finn starts to fuck me and his fingers thread through my hair, massaging my scalp and pulling on my hair in intervals. Rowan mutters curses when I use my tongue to hit every last spot he likes. It's one of my favorite parts about being on my knees for him—that I know exactly what he likes, when he likes it, and I can have him wrapped around my finger in a few moments.

"Fuck, yes. Like that. That's my perfect little whore." Rowan's eyes shutter as he praises me, and I work harder to bring him to the edge as I feel his fingers twist in my hair.

Finn continues to fuck me, his pace picking up and his hands massaging my ass and hips as he works me over, careful to follow the rules and not to do any of things he knows I normally need to come.

I glance over at Hudson and his shirt is off and his pants are undone as he strokes his cock. His tongue darts out over his lip and he squeezes the head of his cock once before he lets go. He runs his hands over his thighs and stretches his fingers trying to distract himself. I can tell how desperate he is to fuck me, and it spurs me on, wanting to give us both our fantasy tonight— knowing how much he loves watching the guys fuck me first.

"Fuck. I'm going to come," Rowan warns a few moments later. "Want me to come on your tongue, Duchess?"

"Only me tonight." Hudson barks out and my eyes snap to his. They're dark with lust and I don't know if Hudson's going to be able to give me the gentle sex he promised earlier. But the Hudson that's picked up tricks from Rowan is just as fun, even if it's a rarer version.

I watch Rowan flash Hudson an annoyed look, but he pulls away from me and I use my hands to finish him off—his eyes closing as he curses through it. Finn lets out a muted groan and pulls out of me a second later, the sound of his hand working his cock before I feel the warmth of him at my back a moment later.

"Fuck me." He groans, his hands sliding over my hips and his thumb rubbing back and forth over my skin as he catches his breath.

Rowan disappears for a moment and returns, handing me one washcloth and another to Finn. Finn cleans me up and then himself and I use the washcloth on my hands and down my neck to cool my skin where I'm flushed from the exertion and the warmth of the fire.

When I look up, Hudson's already standing over me, stripped down and watching me like he's about to consume me the moment he gets his hands on me. I start to get up on my knees, ready to take him in my mouth but he makes a noise.

"Lay back and spread your legs for me. I want to see how wet you are from letting them use you like that. The way you moan and whimper for them—I can barely take how good it is."

I do as he asks, laying back on the rug and letting my thighs fall apart for him. His gaze darkens as his eyes run over my body, landing hard when he sees how wet I am.

"I need you, Hudson."

It's all I have to say and he's on his knees a second later, his face between my thighs as his tongue slides over me, circling my clit before he repeats the process. I whimper and then bite down on lower lip, reaching for him and feeling the softness of his hair against my palm as he devours me. He's so devoted in his task, he barely takes a breath. Not letting up until I'm begging to have him inside me and he finally relents. I turn my head, closing my eyes and trying to catch my own breath as his hands run over every inch of my skin.

His cock teases my clit before he slides inside me. I rock my hips desperate for the friction I need to chase my release. He leans over me, one hand wrapping around the base of my neck while he braces himself with the other. His mouth is just beneath my jaw, and he groans against my skin when he starts to fuck me slowly.

"I love you so much. You're so fucking good to me. I want to feel how hard you come on my cock though, Duchess. Listen to you curse like you hate me." He whispers just loud enough for me to hear.

He delivers on his earlier promise, fucking me slow and steady to torture me before he finally tightens his grip on my neck.

"Give me everything." His tone demanding.

Those words from him are the little push I needed to fall over the edge, and I start to come, cursing and moaning for him as I beg him to finish me off.

"Oh fuck. My sweet girl." He mutters and I hear his breath stutter as his own release hits him hard. He takes me in shallower passes, slowing his rhythm before he pulls out of me and falls down next to me on the rug.

He lays on his back, smiling as he takes deep breaths and then looks over at me.

"See, wasn't that romantic?"

I grin and roll over onto his chest. "Dreadfully so." I kiss his chin, and his hand cups under mine.

"You're so gorgeous, Charlotte. I'm so lucky. *We're* so lucky." His eyes flick up to Rowan and Finn who are collapsed against the couch with heavy lids. Rowan offers the quirk of his brow and Finn gives me a lazy grin.

"Good thing we stole her away," Finn muses.

"Best thing we've ever taken." Hudson grins bright and kisses me.

I smile back at him for a moment and then sit up.

"All right. Showers, then bed. I vote we sleep in."

"Seconded." Hudson agrees with me as he stands. He grabs me a moment later, throwing me over his shoulder as he walks us to the bathroom. "But first, I get to help you shower."

———

When I get out of the bathroom after the guys leave me to finish up, the three of them are lounging around the fireplace with hot cocoa and Finn stands to hand me my own mug.

"Extra marshmallows," he says as he kisses my temple.

"Thank you."

My heart is so full of these three that it's hard to remember a time I wasn't happy anymore.

"You've got some presents to open." Hudson nods at three small boxes on the coffee table as I sit down on the couch between him and Rowan.

"We said we weren't doing gifts this year..." I sigh as I shake my head. "I didn't get you all anything yet."

"It wouldn't have been a surprise otherwise." Rowan kicks his feet up on the table.

"Open them." Finn hands me one of the boxes before he sits down on the chair.

I untie the ribbon and unwrap the Christmas paper, opening the small black box inside. It's a plain silver ring. I glance up Finn, my brow knitting as I study his bemused expression.

"Never seen a ring before?" He smirks.

"I just didn't... I mean..." I stumble over my words and his smirk melts into a smile. He gets out of the chair and kneels down next to me, plucking the ring out of the box and putting it on my left ring finger.

"Now this one." He hands me the next box that's the same size and I open it the same way I did the last. There's another ring inside and I raise a brow.

Hudson leans over and pulls the ring out. He turns it over and lets the light from the fire catch on the engraving on the inside of the ring.

"Girl?" I ask, reading it out loud.

"The one Finn just put on you has one too."

I pull it off and let it catch the light.

"Our girl?" I feel tears start to well up and Hudson kisses my cheek while Finn helps me slip the rings back on.

"Our girl." Finn grins at me.

"Open the last one." Rowan nods to the bigger box and I eye him as I go to reach for it.

When I unwrap it, I find a necklace with a blackberry pendant that sparkles in the light. I turn to look at him, tears starting to fall down my cheeks, and his eyes meet mine for a moment before they dart away again.

"Here." Rowan holds his hand out after he sets his mug down, and I hand him the box.

He pulls the necklace out and then motions for me to turn so he can put it on. He slips it around my neck and hooks the clasp, letting it fall into place. I wrap my fingers around it and glance up at him.

"I love it."

He leans forward, cupping my jaw as he kisses me. It's softer than his usual kiss, gentler in the way his lips pass over mine, like he's trying to kiss the tears away. I melt into his touch for a moment before we pull away. He grabs his mug of cocoa again and I run my fingers over his knee.

"Thank you." I grin at Finn and Hudson. "I love it so much. I wish I could have gotten you something though."

"We have you every day. That's enough." Hudson wraps an arm around me, pulling me close, and I lean against his shoulder, my eyes drifting to Finn.

"Ready for bed?" Finn asks as he stands, holding out his hand. I nod and he hauls me up to my feet. The rest follow us up the stairs.

Before I know it, we're all tucked into the two beds we pushed together in the loft, Hudson snoring and Finn dead to the world at my side. I stare at the vaulted ceiling above me, drifting off to sleep thinking how thankful I am for these three and how Christmas has definitely become my favorite time of year.

―――――

Later that night I wake up and make my way downstairs to get a drink. I look out the window to the massive navy sky dotted with stars and framed by the frost on the windowpanes. I take another sip of the warm apple cider when I feel arms wrap around my waist and lips pressed to my exposed shoulder.

"You didn't wake them up, did you?" I whisper.

"No. Hudson's still snoring like a fucking hibernating bear and Finn didn't even move," Rowan answers, kissing the side of my throat.

"Good. I don't think Finn's had a whole night's sleep since London." I've been worried about him.

"And what about you?" he asks, pointing out the obvious.

"I'm just worried about getting back to the States. Meeting with the courier in Chicago."

"Let me be the one to worry." He presses another kiss to my shoulder.

I glance back at him, raising a brow and giving him a look that tells him these days we both get to worry.

"It's fine, Charlotte. I promise. I've checked and double checked all the papers we had made in Prague. We'll get through."

"I hope so."

"Right now you've just got to enjoy this place. Try to get your mind off of it all. The rest is a problem for another day."

I smirk and flash him another knowing look. "Rich coming from you."

He sighs and kisses the crook of my neck, his fingers straightening my necklace.

"I really do love it. You didn't have to do that." I touch the bauble hanging near my heart.

He takes a deep breath and I feel it dance over my skin on his exhale, surprising me when he speaks again instead of his usual stoic silence.

"You know I couldn't live without you. Couldn't breathe without you. That I'd do anything for you."

"I know..." I give him a wary look because he's never this serious about emotions. "Should I be worried?"

"No. I just... I know I don't always say it. Especially with them around. I just want to make sure you know it. Remember it. Always."

I turn around and place my hand on his chest, studying his face for a moment. His gray eyes intense even in the dull light of the dying fire.

"I know, Rowan. I've always known."

His lips brush over mine softly and he rests his forehead against mine. I lean into him, and his arms wrap around me. We stand like that for a long while, until the wee hours finally start to creep in, and we stumble our way back to bed and I curl up in his arms to fall asleep.

———

Want to be the first to know when the next book in this world is coming? Sign up here: maggierawdon.com/lomupdates/

Also by Maggie Rawdon

Plays & Penalties Series

Pregame - Prequel Short Story

Play Fake - Waylon & Mackenzie

Delay of Game - Liam & Olivia

Personal Foul - Easton & Wren

Reverse Pass - Ben & Violet

Seattle Phantom Football Series

Defensive End - Prequel Short Story

Pick Six - Alexander & Harper

Overtime - Joss & Colt

Wild Card - Tobias & Scarlett

Acknowledgments

To you, the reader, thank you so much for taking a chance on this book and on me! Your support means the world.

To Kat, Vanessa, and SJ - there's no way this book would have happened without you. You know how much I'm in awe of your talent and constant unflagging support of my projects but I still have to put it in print every single time. Thank you for being the best editing team an author could ask for.

To Autumn, thank you for your unflinching support when I told you that I was writing morally grey hockey players instead of the cute football romance we had planned and your continued support even when I doubted myself. I hope the epilogue lives up to your inspiration!

To Emma, Shannon, and Thorunn, thank you for your constant support and enthusiasm for all of my wild ideas and being excited to read this one when I told you I'd gone off script. I couldn't have done this without your encouragement.

To Jenn and Candice, thank you for being amazing beta readers and giving your time and thoughts on this one!

To my Promo Team, thank you so much for all the support you give my characters, books, and me. I wouldn't be able to do this without you and I'm so incredibly grateful!

About the Author

Maggie Rawdon is a sports romance author living in the Midwest. She's writes athletes with the kind of filthy mouths that will make you blush and swoon and the smart independent women that make them fall first. She has a weakness for writing frenemies whose fighting feels more like flirting and found families.

She loves real sports as much as the fictional kind and spends football season writing in front of the TV with her pups at her side. When she's not on editorial deadline you can find her binging epic historical dramas or fantasy series in between weekend hikes.

Join the newsletter here for sneak peeks and bonus content:
https://geni.us/MRBNews
Join the reader's group on FB here:
https://www.facebook.com/groups/rawdonsromanticrebels

instagram.com/maggierawdonbooks
tiktok.com/@maggierawdon
facebook.com/maggierawdon

Manufactured by Amazon.ca
Bolton, ON

36163798R00125